PULLED
BACK

BOOK TWO:
A FLAME REBORN

DANIELLE
BANNISTER

First Edition

For information about permission to reproduce selections from this novel, write to: Danielle Bannister, 18 Morgan Lane, Searsmont, ME 04973

Pulled Back: a novel about twin flames re-connecting.

ISBN: 13-978-1482638424
ISBN: 10-148268428

Cover Design by Kari's Literary Solutions

Acknowledgments

First and foremost, I need to thank the fans of PULLED, without whom, this sequel would never have been written. PULLED had always been, in my mind, a one-shot book. When the fans demanded more, however, it pushed my thinking beyond what I had envisioned and forced me to discover there was more story left to be told. I can only hope you like what you helped me create.

Next, I need to thank my beta readers. Those few dedicated readers went beyond the call of duty, to find what needed to be mended before presenting it to my editing team.

Speaking of which, a big thanks goes out to Jen Wendell and my editor Ansley Kniskern. What would I have done without you two? I'd probably be drowning in commas and semi colons!

And finally, to my husband, Jason, and my kiddos, Tristan and Marina. They, reluctantly, allowed me the time needed to take this journey with you.

Do not stand at my grave and weep.
I am not there, I do not sleep.
I am a thousand winds that blow on the snow.
I am the sunlight that ripened grain.
I am the gentle autumn's rain.
When you awake in the morning's hush, I am the swift uplifting rush;
of quiet birds in circled flight, I am the soft star that shines at night.
Do not stand at my grave and cry.
I am not there.
I did not die.

-An Irish Prayer

Prologue

Friday, October 2011

Brenda's body ached. She'd been scrambling around the nursery wing for the last twelve hours. It was all she could do to keep her eyes open.

In the early morning light at Webster General Hospital, the steady rhythm of three newborn heart monitors filled the quiet halls.

Brenda found herself struggling with the injustices of life. While she had been busy helping the docs with three different mothers who all decided to go into labor at once, on the floor below her, three of the local college kids were dying. From what Brenda heard, it had been brutal. A jealous boyfriend killed his girlfriend and her lover and then killed himself. Brenda didn't know all the details but heard one of the friend's of the deceased talking to a reporter about the tragedy. Three children were taken from this world while three more were getting the chance to start fresh. It was all part of the irony of life.

As she gazed at two of her new charges, she felt ready to drift off to sleep right along with them. That's when she heard her name being shouted from down the hall.

"Brenda!"

Even without looking up, she knew to whom the glottal-fried voice belonged to: Marilyn. Marilyn was a scrawny, white woman who had teeth too big for her mouth and a nose ready to stick into any place it didn't belong.

"You off?" Marilyn asked, leaning against the counter as Brenda pulled on her sweater.

"Yup. Been a wild night with these two," Brenda replied, gesturing toward the glass wall behind her that held Jada and Tobias: her two lovebirds.

Marilyn craned her neck to look at the infants.

"I thought you had three of them. What did you do? Lose one?"

Brenda frowned. Hawk (of all things to name a child) had yet to join Jada and Tobias in the nursery. That suited Brenda just fine. There was something she just couldn't put her finger on behind that boy's pale blue eyes. They made her shiver whenever she caught a glimpse of them.

Ignoring Marilyn, Brenda focused her gaze on baby Jada and said a silent prayer for her mama who was upstairs in the O.R. after hemorrhaging during the delivery. Although the odds were grim, Brenda still prayed her hardest. A girl needs her mama. Without one, a woman grows up not feeling whole.

It gave Brenda great comfort to know that, for now, baby Jada had little Tobias to keep her company. Her heart swelled when she looked at the two of them. They were both swaddled and snug in their blankets, their tiny faces pressed close to the thin layer of plastic that kept them apart. Oh, how Brenda wanted to remove that single barrier and allow them to snuggle up to each other as they so clearly wanted to do, but she couldn't. There were policies that forced her hands into submission.

At least those two weren't crying anymore. Brenda only wished she had figured out why they had been so upset sooner. She might not have suffered with the headache she got as a result of their unhappiness.

After all, who would have ever guessed what would have stopped their cries? The very idea was ridiculous.

When Brenda had first placed them in the nursery, she thought she'd give the two of them a little distance, thinking they might wake each other up. So, she put Tobias on one end of the nursery and Jada on the other. That had been a *big* mistake. There was an all out riot by those infants with screams of agony so powerful and inconsolable that it had actually scared Brenda. Nothing in her 20 year arsenal of pediatric nursing seemed to calm those babies down until, quite by accident, another nurse came in to help. She had merely picked up Tobias and walked over to Brenda, who was trying her best to hush Jada, when both babies suddenly stopped crying and started cooing.

She still couldn't believe it. What those two babies wanted, even more than the milk in their bottles, was each other. They just wanted to be close to one another. It was, by far, the strangest thing, she had ever witnessed.

Brenda worried what the parents might think when they would have to be separated the next day. They'd probably claim those babies were just colicky when really they would just be longing for the other.

Brenda chuckled to herself. She'd been reading too many romance novels.

Reluctantly, she turned her attention back to Marilyn whose eyes were pinched close in disgust as she peered into the nursery.

"Not much to that runt, is there?"

"Tobias," Brenda corrected firmly. "And he ain't no runt. He's perfect just the way God made him."

Marilyn scoffed. "I give that boy a year."

Heat bubbled inside of Brenda, filling her cheeks. A protective rage she didn't realize she even possessed washed over her. Her fists clenched as she tried to contain herself.

"No one wants the runt of a litter," Marilyn continued, oblivious to Brenda's fuming. "That's probably why his folks are putting him up for adoption."

All the fire drained out of Brenda and was replaced with shock. "What?"

Marilyn shrugged her shoulders without compassion. "I heard the dad talking on the phone to someone about it."

So, that's why no one had been knocking down the nursery door to see Tobias. They didn't plan on getting attached. Tears crept into the corners of her eyes.

"Things aren't looking good for that girl's mamma, either." Marilyn pointed her cotton candy pink nail toward Jada. "I just had to bring a crash cart into her room. The dad's an absolute mess."

It's times like this that Brenda hated her job. She knew better than to get attached to those who come here, and yet, she found herself doing it every day, more so today than ever before. Angry at the injustice of it all, Brenda turned away from Marilyn and pushed her way into the nursery. The click of the door closing behind her echoed into the hollows of her heart.

Tears blurred Brenda's vision, but she found her way over to Tobias and Jada, gently pressing a hand on each of their precious little bodies. They were still cooing at each other, blissfully unaware of how much their happy little lives would change.

Chapter 1

September 2029

Jada

The final drop of blood lands in the pink-tinged bathwater around me.

About time! I hiss at myself, annoyed that it took longer than normal for my blood to clot. Most days it only takes a couple minutes for the bleeding to stop, but today I had to carve the letter 'J.' Because of the curve, it's trickier to keep the blade still. The built up scar tissue doesn't make it any easier.

As I wipe away the last traces of the blood from the tub, It dawns on me that I've been etching my name into my forearm for almost ten years. You'd think I'd be used to the pain at this point. Or, at the very least, that my body would refuse to bleed at all. But the fire burns each and every time. As it should. After all, pain is better than forgetting who I am. Or rather, who I'm *not*.

I am not my mother, no matter how many times my father calls me her name in his drunken rages. I etch a letter into my flesh every day to keep some small part of me whole, a painful reminder that I'm still alive and she is dead.

Inside my room, I turn on the one overhead light and pull the curtain that is my door closed. Mechanically, I tie on the black leather band I use to hide the cuts. The rough leather against my raw flesh burns as I tie it tight to my skin. It always amuses me how people think it's just an 'Urban Goth' accessory.

In keeping with the facade, I pull on torn leggings and a tank top, black, of course, (wouldn't want to mess with their assumptions now, would I?). The boots go on last before I try my best to tiptoe down the stairs, hoping not to be seen. Instead, I am greeted with the sound of my dad's oh-so-eloquent cursing. *Lovely.*

He grunts, hunched under the sink, tinkering with it. Again. *Oh, he's gonna be in a great mood today.* I walk over to one of the kitchen cabinets and pull out two cups for coffee, not because I'm daughter-of-the-year, but because it's expected. The fewer ripples I make in my dad's day, the better off we all are.

Plopping down on the counter, I hover over the machine, willing it to do whatever it does faster. *Stupid, ancient, piece of junk!* When I move outta here, I am *so* getting an Insta Brew, even if I have to sell a kidney to buy it. I only need one kidney to survive, right?

While I wait I breathe in the caffeinated

aroma, which helps bring me to life. Some days, coffee is the only thing I live for. No joke.

My father and I have a unique relationship. We each do our best to ignore the others existence. Most days, it's easy. He wakes up, usually hung over, then finds some sort of work to pay for the rent and his booze. I do my best to stay out of his way. It's win-win, really. Nine times out of ten, he doesn't even remember I live here. It's the tenth day you gotta watch out for. Those are days he remembers that I'm alive and his beloved wife isn't.

He's been sober-ish for about a month now as far as I can tell. He seemed to stop drinking when he made the choice to move back to Mom's home town. I don't expect it to last. But I haven't seen the vodka bottles piling up yet. I avoid him though, just in case, because, let's be honest. There are mean drunks, and then there is my dad.

The coffee finally coughs out 'its last drop from the blasted machine, so I start adding several artificial flavor packets in a feeble attempt to make it taste palatable. Obviously, because of my dad's work ethic, we can't afford the real beans, but still, this artificial crap is just wrong. It's like giving tofu to tigers.

As the powder dissolves, I look down at my dad's butt hanging out of his pants and start an imaginary conversation with the shell of a father I have:

"Only two more days until school starts, Jada lamb. You excited?"

"I sure am, Dad! I can't wait to start my senior year."

"I'm so proud of you, hun. I wish your mother was alive to see this."

I sigh to myself. *That talk will never happen, Jada. Keep dreaming.*

Jumping off the counter, I try not to think about school, cause let's face it: schools are cruel, especially to the newbies. I should know. I've started nine different schools so far. Each move promised a new beginning and each one fell flat. It didn't matter where we went, there would always be some random thing that reminded Dad of *her*. Of the life he had before I screwed it up. Then his depression would return, the vodka would come out, something bad would happen and we would have to move. It was the circle of my life.

I don't blame him for who he turned into. I should, but I don't. I blame people's ridiculous obsession with love. It's unhealthy and unrealistic. People who believe in love are nothing short of brainwashed. They've been made to think the fairytale is real. But, I know the truth: love is a lie mankind made up to give us hope for something, *anything*, better than what we are.

Setting my cup down, I move over to the fridge to scavenge for breakfast. The selection is limited, to say the least. "So much for eating," I grumble to myself.

"I've got a job this morning over at Ms. Philips' place," Dad yells, from under the sink. "Her hot water heater kicked the bucket last night."

That may be the longest sentence he's ever said to me.

"Okay," I say, slipping out of the back door.

It's better not to engage in conversation with him if I can avoid it.

Outside, I sneak a peak over to Ms. Philips' trailer. Her place doesn't look any better than ours, so I wonder if she will actually have the cash to pay for the repairs. She *does*, however, own a car. Something we haven't had in years. Once gas prices hit nine dollars a gallon in 2020, Dad sold the truck and we've relied on public transportation ever since. Too bad there isn't any here in Webster. Maybe having a neighbor with a car will come in handy.

Annoyed, I start walking to school to register for classes. If I'm going to survive here in the boondocks, I guess I'm gonna have to learn how to hoof it.

Tobias

"Tobs!" I hear my name being called the second I step out of the shower. Water drips off onto the green, cracked tile floor. "Get your ass out here and help me bag this bird before your mom comes home and skins me alive!" I shake my head. It's Hawk. If he wasn't my best friend, I swear I'd have to hit him.

I grab a threadbare towel and wrap it around my waist. Prying open the swollen windowsill, I duck my head out. Just as I do, an arrow lodges itself deep into the wooden frame beside me— inches from my face.

I rip my head back, banging it against the sill. "Damn it, Hawk! You could have hit me," I shout down at him, feeling my head for a lump.

He gives me an mischievous smile. "If I had wanted to hit you, I would have. Want me to prove it?" He aims his bow at my head and I duck. Although I know he's kidding, his aim is lethal.

"Will you stop? My mom's coming home in, like thirty minutes," I yell.

"Exactly, so get your butt down here!" he shouts back at me.

I shake my head, knowing he won't stop pestering me until he gets what he wants. Hawk has a way of doing that. It pisses me off sometimes. "Hang on," I tell him. "Let me get some clothes on!" I yank the arrow out of the frame and toss it down to Hawk who catches it before it lands. I pull the window back down and feel the welt on my head. *Damn.*

Still dripping wet, I climb over piles of dirty clothes and balled up wads of used tissues. I've been hacking up a lot of junk lately and have been too tired to clean up. I sneak a puff off my inhaler and feel my lungs expand. *Stupid asthma.*

I rummage through the options I have to wear, sniffing around for what is the least offensive. I was supposed to do the laundry this morning, but I slept in, which is odd for me. Normally, I'm up with the sun, but today. I don't feel all that great. Not that there is anything unusual about that. I never feel one hundred percent, but lately my asthma has been getting worse. I'm hoping it's just because of the change in seasons and not what I think it is. I'm living on borrowed time with this diseased lung. If my name doesn't get chosen for a donor soon... well, let's just say Hawk will have to learn how to hunt on his own.

Downstairs, I pocket my inhaler and pop a neon yellow allergy tab. I miss the old-school pill form I used to take when I was a kid. At least with those you didn't have to endure the acidic taste as it dissolves on your tongue.

I run my hands through my chaotic dark curls in a pathetic effort to style my hair and then swipe a toothbrush across my less than perfect teeth. I frown at my reflection. I'm not an ugly dude, I'm just not the type of guy anyone would ever mistake for Hawk, especially with this gaunt, sick look I've got going on.

As soon as I get down the porch steps, Hawk throws my bow at me, which I don't manage to catch. My fingers fumble to grasp the string, but I just end up looking like an idiot when I miss. He laughs at me.

"Not cool, man. Not cool," I say bending down and grabbing the bow he made for me last year. Since neither one of us can legally buy weapons until next year, we have resorted to making them. Well, he made them. I just use them--poorly.

"I spotted a rafter of turkeys just over the hill," Hawk says, gesturing over his shoulder. "There's one that looks slow enough for even you to hit." He punches me lightly on the arm and it almost knocks me over.

"Ha, ha," I mumble, slinging the bow over my shoulder.

Hawk's blond head disappears into the woods, barely making a sound as I bumble behind him, trying to keep up. Hawk is a natural born hunter. His tracking instincts are like nothing I've ever seen. The look he gets in his eyes when he's hunting is downright scary sometimes.

It's almost like the hunt takes over his brain. Guess it's better to hunt *with* him than to be the subject of his tracking skills.

Hawk runs up the hill in front of us with such speed and stealth it makes my head spin. I do my best to follow close behind, but my lungs begin to struggle as I crest the hill, forcing me to steal a puff off my inhaler; a sound which earns a 'shh' from Hawk.

"Sorry," I whisper. "Trying to stay alive here."

"Yeah, well, do it quieter." He points through a break in the trees.

Just as he predicted, the turkeys are there, milling around in the field, unaware that their days are numbered. The turkeys bob their heads back and forth, plucking at the over grown hay field. The morning fog covers all but the tops of their heads, but I know Hawk can see every detail on their feathered bodies. My heart starts to race in my chest. Hunting turkeys is highly illegal now that they are endangered, which, of course, is the only reason why Hawk wants to hunt them.

Hawk lets out a small sigh, clearly getting off from the rush of the hunt. He raises his bow and signals for me to do the same. When I try to pull the string back, the muscles in my arm scream. I curse at myself. Just last week I pulled this back with no problem, but now...

He looks over his shoulder at me. "You okay?" He whispers.

I release the string and drop the arrow to the ground. "I've been better."

His face grows dark. He hates it when I get sick. He always has. Even in kindergarten he'd follow me around on the playground making sure

I didn't run or overexert myself. And he'd gladly beat up any kid who tried to tease me. I honestly don't think I could have made it this long without him.

Hawk turns his attention back to the turkeys and fires a single shot. Even without looking, I know he's hit his target. Hawk never misses.

"Sit," Hawk orders after he's released his string, and I do, grateful for the tree stump a few feet away. "Rest. I'll be right back," he tells me. I feel like such a pansy getting winded after climbing up one stupid hill, but the way my body feels right now, resting is all I *can* do.

The mist feels like sandpaper against my lungs, wearing them down. I take a few more puffs off my inhaler to quell the pain. I do my best to focus my breathing into slow, steady inhalations. That's the only thing that makes the pain subside. Eventually, my lungs begin to expand just enough to allow me to take a few small, shallow breaths.

Hawk emerges from the field a few minutes later carrying the biggest turkey I've ever seen. The neck of the bird is wrapped securely in his hands. Placing it on the ground beside me, he yanks the arrowhead out and wipes the blood from its tip onto the ground without even flinching.

"Too bad we can't eat the damn thing," he says, before tossing the bird out into the woods for some lucky scavenger to snatch. Bringing the bird home would get both of our asses cooked.

Turkeys have only been on the endangered list a year or so. After we lost the last bald eagle to pollution five years ago, the government started cracking down hard on hunting turkeys, our new national bird. The turkey. *So proud to be an American.*

Hawk plops down beside me and runs his hands through his sun-bleached hair, something he does when he's nervous. "Dumbo off your chest yet?"

I nod. I've told him before that having an asthma attack is like having an elephant sit on your lungs while you are still trying to breathe-- through a straw.

"I feel like crap today," I confess.

"You look like it, too."

"Thanks, bro."

Hawk leans back against an oak tree and begins to clean the blood out from under his nails with the arrowhead he carved out of stone. "You can't go and die on me, you know. It's our senior year."

I give him a weak smile. "Right. My bad."

"Seriously, man. You okay?"

I'm not really sure how to answer him. I want to give him the traditional 'I'm fine,' but he knows I'm not. Maybe I am finally reaching the point the docs told me should have come years ago. With pollution as bad as it is, treatments for asthma have grown less and less effective. It really is some kind of scientific miracle that I was still alive.

"I don't know." It's the best I have.

Hawk snaps his head up, listening to something.

"Well, you might bite it before school even starts," Hawk says. "Your mom's home."

He's right. Mom's ride just pulled into the

driveway.

I curse under my breath. "She's early. Quick, hide the bows," I say, yanking mine off my shoulder and tucking it behind the tree next to me.

Hiding the bows is probably not necessary since no one comes into our backyard but us, but it's better to be safe than in jail.

When we're satisfied with our hiding job, we head inside. Mom has planted herself in the living room, where it looks like she just collapsed onto the couch. Her scrubs (that she'd ironed meticulously this morning) now hang wrinkled against her slumped shoulders.

"Long day?" I ask, smiling down at her.

"Don't ask," she says. One of her dark gray dreadlocks has fallen out of her elastic band, but she doesn't seem to care. She looks beyond tired. I feel bad that she's still working at her age. She could have retired last year but, with my medical bills, she had to stay on. Once I'm out of school, I'm gonna make her quit. I'll find a job and take over my own bills. She's cared for me far longer than a mother should have to.

"Good morning, Ms. Garret," Hawk says, walking in from the kitchen.

"It's night for me," Mom says, rubbing her red eyes. "Lord, these twelve-hour shifts are killing me."

"Go to bed, I'll wake you for dinner," I say, trying to yank her off of the couch and force her to bed.

"Can't. I've gotta get you registered for school today." She bats my arm away and pulls herself up off our beat-up couch.

"Ma, I can register myself for school. I *am* a senior now." Underclassmen have to have a parent register them, but not seniors. We are considered old enough to handle this ridiculous privilege on our own.

She shakes her head no. "I don't want you walking that far by yourself. The smog count is supposed to climb later today." Her voice is tired but still has that tone of authority in it. I won't sway her. Not on my own.

Without me having to say a word, Hawk knows just what to do.

"I'll go with him," Hawk says. "You know I won't let anything happen to him." He gives her his best shit-eating grin. I actually see Mom falling for it. And why wouldn't she? She's a sucker when it comes to Hawk. Everyone is.

Although, when we first started hanging out as kids, Ma couldn't get over the color of his eyes. It freaked her out. Eventually, though, his charm won her over. Hawk's a slick one.

Ma's relenting sigh tells me we've won. "Bring your e-thingy and your inhaler."

"They are called e-portals, Ma, and I've already got both on me," I say, looping my arm through hers. The contrast of her black skin next to my overtly pale skin always surprises me a bit. I know that I'm adopted, but I guess I just forget sometimes. Maybe that's because, to me, she's always just been Mom.

In our puny kitchen, she gives each of us a quick peck on the head before she labors up the narrow stairs. She leans against the wood paneling as she climbs, proof of how tired she is. I hate that she works so hard.

When she's out of earshot, Hawk gives me a cautious look.

"You sure you're up for this?"

"So long as you don't mind carrying me on the way back," I say, smiling, only half-kidding.

"You got it," he says, giving me a light punch on the arm before we start walking toward the school.

Chapter 2

Jada

Walking, like mornings, suck. I've been schlepping down this road for a good half-hour and the school is just now coming into view. *Ten minutes, my ass.* There is no way I'm gonna pull this trip off twice a day. Not without some serious complaining and a huge cup of coffee.

Irritated, and now gross and sweaty, I make my way up the steps to the brick school. The mortar is cracking and the windows need paint. The place is probably full of mold, too.

I rip off the elastic that is holding my hair back. The thick strands have managed to mat themselves together at the nape of my neck. My fingers comb through the mess in a feeble attempt to tame the sweaty knots. God, I hate summer. And winter. And most of spring.

When I finally manage to find the office in this joint, there is already a line that wraps the length of the hall. *Lovely.* Looking down the line, I roll my eyes. Most of the kids are underclassman. They're all glued tight to their doting parents. All the parental love in the air makes me want to hurl.

Sighing, I plop down on the floor to wait. I fish out my refurbished e-portal (that I saved up every penny I ever made to get) and select the 'radio' icon. A graphic of an old-school i-Pad flashes on my screen. Those ancient things were worthless. You couldn't even scan your groceries with them! Back in my dad's day, you had to pay for things, like food, with real money. Gross. I can't even imagine handling a piece of paper that hundreds of other people have touched.

That's probably why they went digital. For awhile there, people were dropping like flies. It was staph infection, from what the teachers tell us. Germs got too strong for us. I can't help but think maybe it was better for the planet that so many died. As it is, we are running out of everything: oil, wood, coffee beans. The world is going to shit. As is the rest of my day, it seems.

Focusing back onto my e-portal, an oval screen pops up notifying me that there is 'a weather emergency.' Clicking on the 'more info' tab, the screen fills with the face of a grim looking reporter next to a man in a green EnviroTech lab coat and that clichéd, slicked back hair. He looks like the poster boy for science.

"This threat is very real," the talking lab coat is saying. "Storm systems moving across the Pacific Ocean are currently carrying some of the toxic chemicals released in last week's nuclear power plant meltdown in North Korea. The storms will likely produce not only compromised breathable air, but potentially high levels of acid rain as well. The EPA is urging everyone to find adequate shelter in the next few days. Adequate shelter meaning: an indoor space with no open windows and oxygen tanks for the elderly and those with breathing issues. We're also urging people to stay tuned to their local news as we track this system for further recommendations."

The warnings continue to rage on the tiny screen as the people in front of me start moving forward, forcing me to get off my butt and move. I had contented myself with being able to stay out of the sun for the rest of the day, but now it looks like I'll be kicked out before lunch. Figures.

At least this means I'll be able to get home before the mid-day sun hits. Not having AC is the pits. *So is not having any damn food,* my stomach grumbles. For a moment, I allow myself to daydream about how excellent a nice, cold slice of cheesecake would feel sliding down my throat right about now. Thick, rich and full of yummy fatty goodness. I can almost remember the last time I had it. Almost.

Tobias

Hawk deliberately walks slowly beside me to school with me in a comfortable silence. He pretends to soak up the sun, but he's really dragging his feet just so I won't have to exert myself. He's always been able to tell when I am hurt or not feeling great.

For example, when we were ten, I was in the hospital for one of my many lung infections and it was pretty hit or miss. I actually slipped into a coma. Docs wanted to pull the plug on me but

Hawk convinced them all that I'd be waking up the next day (which I did). He said he could sense it. He told everyone he knew I'd wake up because I told him I would. Of course, I don't remember any of that, but he swears I spoke to him while I was under. We're connected in some freaky way. It's more than just your average best friend stuff, at least according to him.

To an outsider, we do make for an unlikely pair. Hawk is the model beefcake, and I'm, well-- not. I think most people just assume Hawk hangs out with me because we're neighbors or because he feels sorry for me. But, it's more than that. We're friends.

Hawk could be really popular if he wanted to be, but he doesn't. He ignores them all; the girls especially. It drives them nuts. Every year, a gaggle of them try to bring him over to the dark side and every time he turns them down flat. When they ask him why he won't date them, he just smiles and says he's waiting for 'the one.' He's not kidding either. He really *is* convinced there is a girl, one *specific* girl, waiting for him out there. He thinks she is all alone and longing for him to find her. So, basically–he's nuts.

As we approach the school doors, Hawk looks at me. A small grin creeps across his face. He's planning something. I can see his brain spinning.

"After we register, let's get breakfast. On me. Gram's birthday e-card got deposited in my account early." He wiggles his eyebrows at me. "I'm rich."

His smile is infectious. I can't help but laugh. "Too bad it may be more like lunch time before we get out of here," I sigh. The registration line is always long. Not because the school is big or anything. There are only a few hundred kids, but they never staff this day properly. No budget, they claim. I think it's more that no one wants to do it.

Hawk drapes his arm around my shoulders and shakes his head at me.

"Let me take care of our registration and grab our forms while you get us a table," he says. "Aunt Trudy is scanning in the office today. She'll let me cut the line, then you and I can get some real grub."

My lungs could use a bit of a break after that walk. Yet, something is nagging at me to stay here.

Before I can protest, however, Hawk rips my registration card out of my hand and starts running past those standing in line. I'd never catch up now, and he knows it. Slouching my shoulders, I kick at the ground and head for the restaurant--as instructed.

Jada

The office lady's nails click on the glass counter a few feet in front of me. Her patience is obviously wearing thin waiting for me to come over to her. So, nice girl that I am, I take my sweet-ass time getting to her. She doesn't scare me with her big hair and too white teeth. It's not my fault they have an archaic registration process that she's forced to operate on one of the last days of summer. No way am I going to let her take out her frustrations with the system on me. I'm just as much of a victim of it as she is. Ever so slowly,

I pull out my registration card from my bag. I'm about to hand it to her when, from out of nowhere, this *guy* just waltzes past me and takes my spot. The spot I'd been waiting over an hour for.

Oh, hell, no!

"Hey! No cutting, jerk."

The fiend turns to look at me. He's a big guy. Not bad on the eyes: yummy, dirty-blond hair that begs to be played with and rock hard pecs pressing against his too tight shirt. Gorgeous. But still...it doesn't give him the right to be an ass.

Blond beauty looks me up and down, amused. I can see him take in my attire: torn black leggings, black tank, combat boots and dark eye liner. I harden myself against his prejudice. *Judgmental prick.* I straighten my shoulders giving my scrawny frame another full inch and give him my best 'don't mess with me' glare. The clothes may be a ruse but he doesn't need to know that. I figure he's about to write me off as just another punk kid, when his expression shifts to intrigue. It's a look I don't get often. It's a look that says, *you think you're hiding...but I see you.*

I do my best to ignore his perfect cool blue eyes, but they stare at me with such intensity that it's hard to pull away. I actually have to blink my way out of his arrogant charm.

"Are you deaf?" I ask, with more venom than I mean. "I said, no cutting."

"Don't forget the 'jerk' part." A sly grin spreads across his perfect little lips.

"My apologies. Jerk."

His smile doesn't even flinch, it just gets

wider. He's pleased with my reply and that ticks me off. I don't want him to like me. I want him to move the hell out of my way.

He leans against the counter and looks at Nail Lady. "Well, I've been called worse. Haven't I, Aunt Trudy?"

Aunt Trudy?

"And not just by me," his aunt replies, with no shred of humor.

Now I feel like the ass, and I'm not even sure why.

Undeterred, he stretches out his hand to me. "I'm Hawk."

"Hawk?" I blink. "Like the bird?" No way this guy's name is Hawk. He's yanking my chain.

"Blame her sister, not me," he says, tilting his head at his aunt who just shrugs her shoulders at me.

His hand is still outstretched, waiting for mine.

Relenting, I take it. His hand almost swallows mine whole. I'm surprised by how cool it is. The shock of his touch zings through me, landing like a punch to the gut. Warning bells go off in my head.

"Look, I'm sorry," I mumble, yanking my hand away as though stung. Instinctively, I fold my hands behind my back. "It's just--I've been waiting a long time."

"No, I get it. Please, after you." He gestures for me to go ahead of him as though he's doing me a favor. I step in front of him. As I do, I swear I can feel his eyes on my backside. To test my paranoia, I glance over my shoulder and sure enough, there he is, gawking away at my lower half. The look on his face is like he's claiming it as his own. *Sorry, buddy*. This chick's not for sale. *Ever.*

His aunt takes my registration card and runs it through her scanner. It uploads my class schedule and e-forms my dad will need to thumbprint his permission on. I'll do it for him one night when he's asleep. He'd never do it on his own.

When Nail Lady finally finishes with me, I gather my stuff and turn around. Mr. Greek God is still there, flashing his pearly whites at me. Obviously this is meant to impress me. *Please.* I'm not gonna fall for his trap. Still, I don't want to make enemies with someone like him, so I give him my best attempt at a smile.

"Thank you," I say, before plowing past him.

"Hey, wait!" He takes my wrist, unknowingly grabbing hold of my leather cuff and the cuts beneath it. I swallow the pain, glare down at his hand and then back at him, eyebrows raised to the sky. He lets go. *Good boy.*

"Look, I'm sorry," he says. He flings two registration cards at his aunt before he turns back to me. By now my arms are firmly crossed over my chest. I don't know what this guy's deal is.

"I was a prick back there," he says. "Sometimes I forget that, just because my aunt works here, it doesn't mean I own the place."

He ducks his chin to his chest and looks at me with the saddest excuse of puppy dog eyes I've ever seen. He must really think I'm a dope if he thinks I'm gonna fall for that. I roll my eyes at him before I start for the door.

"Wait! Let me make it up to you. I'm about to have a late breakfast with my buddy. Come with us. My treat. Please?"

The request is so random that I actually find myself stopping to contemplate it. My stomach does a small grumble and I hope he doesn't hear. Still, I don't know this guy, so no dice.

"Thanks, but I'll pass."

My feet make quick yet clumpy strides down the hall and I curse myself for wearing these stupid boots.

"They have *real* coffee!" he shouts after me.

I stop in mid-clomp. Slowly, I turn around. I can't help myself. "Really?"

"Really." His eyes twinkle.

Okay, maybe I am crazy to go somewhere with a perfect stranger but real coffee is real coffee. Sometimes a girl's just gotta take a risk.

Chapter 3

Tobias

The breakfast rush at Nathan's Bistro hasn't started yet, so I'm able to snag the corner booth with the killer view of the woods. The trees are just now starting to change. In a month, those big old maples will turn this town into a tourist's dream. Until then, the locals claim the booth.

As I slide in, I can't help but brush my fingers over the worn leather that covers the seats. The hairline scars etched into its deep mahogany skin speaks volumes of the abuse it's gone through over the years. That's why this is my favorite spot. I love its history.

The host drops the two menus I asked for and then disappears around the corner without so much as a hello. Not that I expect one. People don't know how to talk to the dying.

I open the menu even though I already know what I am going to order. The house special: the American cheddar omelet, home fries and the biggest chai in the county. Hawk will get the flapjacks, extra sausage, a side of hash and a glass of egg yolks. Gross.

Across from me, a couple of waiters busy themselves by making fresh napkin rolls. Their fingers move like lightning as they roll the silver inside the red cloths. They make it look so easy.

Glancing down at my own utensil roll, I unravel it. The pieces clink together in objection. I make a few halfhearted attempts of my own at rolling them back together like they do, but I can't seem to achieve the crispness the roll originally had. I frown. Unrollers remorse. I push the mess aside, frustrated.

It's while I'm putting my hand down in my lap that I notice it. The tiny hairs on my arm are all starting to stand on end. It's more than just a chill. It's like each one of my hairs is being pulled straight up by something. Freaking out, I look around to other customers, assuming there must be some sort of electrical storm happening or something, but no one else seems to be afflicted by whatever is happening to me.

I glance back down at my arm. The hairs are completely erect now. *What the hell?* I try to brush them down, but they refuse to lay flat no matter what I do. That's when the oddest sense of *deja vu* comes over me. I swear I've tried to push down these stubborn hairs a hundred times before.

Panic hits me. Maybe I *am* getting sick?

As I feel my forehead for a sign of a fever, a wave of something hauntingly familiar hits me. Lilac. It's way too late in the year for lilacs, but it's lilac all right. I should know--I'm allergic to it. Methodically, I start to dig out my inhaler, but stop because the urge to cough is absent, which doesn't make any sense. If that really is lilac I'm smelling, I should be coughing my head off right now.

I close my eyes to try and calm down, but that's when I'm assaulted by an image so strong, it almost knocks me out of the booth. In my head, I see a pale looking girl with jet black hair and the kindest eyes I've ever seen. She looks so familiar to me. It's her smile though, that unglues me. A smile that is filled with such love and tenderness-- it actually hurts to look at her. A name screams in my head: *Naya!*

Then, just as fast as it came, the face fades away, leaving my heart feeling oddly hollow.

Okay, who the hell was that?

Opening my eyes, the business of the restaurant has come back into focus, leaving no trace of the vision I left behind.

I rub my temples, trying to get a grip on what I just saw. The host flies by my table, almost knocking my elbow off the edge. My eyes follow him as he makes his way around the corner to greet some new arrivals. Everything seems back to normal.

But then, just as before, everything shifts in the blink of an eye. As soon as the host disappears, my muscles tense up, locking me in place. Instantly, my heart begins to hammer out a staccato rhythm in anticipation. *But anticipation of what? Of who!* my head shouts back at me.

The tightness builds in my throat and doesn't let up one iota as the seconds drag by. My stomach is tying itself into huge knots waiting for *something* to happen. It's almost like everything is going in slow motion.

By the time the host rounds the corner to

seat his next table, I can barely breathe. That's when Hawk emerges from behind him. He's wearing a big goofy grin. Seeing Hawk is almost like a punch to the gut. He isn't who I'm waiting for which made no sense. *Who else did I think would be coming?*

That's when *she* appears.

This stranger walking next to Hawk that I swear I've met a millions times before.

I can't help but think that she reminds me of the girl I just saw in my head, except she is her exact opposite. The girl walking toward me with her shoulders slumped is not the confident and kind-eyed girl I just daydreamed about. And yet, her face is so painfully familiar that it makes my body shake.

Who is she?

Hawk's wave grabs my attention, but I can't seem to tear my eyes away from the girl with him. With each step she takes towards me, my chest responds by inching itself forward. I am like a moon succumbing to her orbit.

When I feel my butt start to slide out of the booth, presumably to get closer to her, I grab the edge of the table in an effort to anchor my body down. The muscles in my forearms   fight against the pressure I have to exude in order to stay in my seat.

What the hell is going on?

Helpless, I watch her come closer from my locked position. She is, quite honestly, the most beautiful girl I have ever seen in my entire life, even though I can barely see her. She's got her head down on the ground, and she's shrouded herself in dark clothes as though she's hiding.

Her golden tendrils obscure half of her face but, even without seeing her, I am undone. I can't help but wonder if this is what Hawk meant about finding 'the one' because right now, I *know* my life will never be the same.

That's when Hawk links his arm into hers. It makes my blood steam. Intense rage bubbles beneath the surface; rage towards my best friend.

Whoa. Calm down, dude!

Hawk doesn't seem to notice my uncalled for hostility as he saunters up to the table with his catch.

"Tobs, this is," he stops and looks at her. "Wait, I didn't catch your name." Hawk laughs.

My mystery girl bites the edge of her lip, and I have to resist the insane desire to kiss the spot she just bit.

"That's because I didn't throw it," she says as those soft lips turn into a hard line.

"Okay, that's fine." Hawk smiles. "Remain a mystery, but I warn you, I love a challenge." He winks at her and I grunt at him in annoyance.

"No Name, this is my friend, Tobs." Hawk says, gesturing my way, clearly not picking up on how much I want to rip his throat out.

"My name's Tob*ias*," I hiss. "Not Tobs." The hostility pours out of me and it scares me. This is not like me.

"Right. Sorry, man." He gives me a look like he really *is* sorry before he gestures for her to sit. She slides into the booth and Hawk swoops in right beside her, caging her in.

Exhaling slowly, I grasp the seat again. I feel the leather buckle and crack from the pressure my fingers make against it, but I'm helpless to stop. I'm suddenly terrified by what I might do if I let go.

"I was a total prick to her at school." Hawk says. "So I'm making it up to her by buying her breakfast."

"You weren't a *total* prick," she replies. The gentle sound of her voice reverberates inside my head. Its familiarity causes such an intense pressure against my chest that I find myself struggling to form coherent thoughts.

Foolishly, I risk a look in her direction. It's like she is calling to me from across the table. When she finally raises her head to meet my gaze, I am rendered speechless. Swept away into a world of nothing but her. It's those *eyes*! They're like the color of melted cocoa, so deep and lush. I've never seen eyes as rich and intense as hers. I am literally hypnotized as they grow wide to look at me—into me.

She is going to be the end of me.

Jada

When Tobias' eyes land on mine, I freeze. I am lost somewhere between the present and past. Memories I know I've never had wash over me, forcing my lids shut. In my mind, I see only dark lips caressing mine. I can clearly make feel a soft tongue slipping inside my mouth, making me moan. A second image flashes before I can process the first: a scar faced boy smiling at me with Tobias' eyes.

Blushing ten shades of scarlet, I rip my lids open only to find Tobias still looking at me. This frail-looking boy (that I've never met) is gazing at me with so much heat that it feels like my insides might just melt. A need like I've never experienced before touches my heart.

Etash! A voice inside my head shouts.

Who? My heart starts hammering, but no one seems to notice.

"So," Hawk says beside me, taking me away from the torment of Tobias' eyes. "Did you just move to Webster or is it really possible that I've not noticed you until now?"

Nothing like a cheesy pick-up line to bring a girl back to her senses. *Does this crap really work with other girls?* A lock of his choppy hair tumbles deliciously across his forehead. Yeah. They fall for it. And why wouldn't they? The guy *is* seriously hot. Too bad he knows it.

"I moved here last month. My dad was... relocated for work," I say, hoping they'd believe the slight exaggeration. Because, let's be honest, my version of the truth that's so much easier than what really happened: *Actually, we move all the time because my dad's a drunken basket case ever since I killed my mom coming out of her womb. Pass the syrup?* See? My version is better.

"It must suck having to start at a new school," Hawk says, leaning in closer to me.

I shrug. "I'm used to it. We move a lot." I hear the sadness in my own voice and it infuriates me. The last thing I want is anyone's pity.

"Well, at least you have friends now, right?" Hawk reaches over the table and smacks Tobias' shoulder with the edge of his menu causing Tobias to flinch. Bully.

The waiter comes and takes our orders. I

mumble out what I think is coffee and eggs, but I can't be sure. I'm too focused on the boy sitting across from me. My brain is insisting that I need to look at Tobias. It's demanding that I remember the taste of his lips on mine.

Whoa. This is freaky.

Using all my strength, I force my eyes to look at Hawk. It's safer to look at Hawk. There's no risk of getting lost in his eyes.

"So, how long have you two known each other?" I ask Hawk, even though my body stays stubbornly rooted toward Tobias.

Hawk sits up in his seat and grins. I return the biggest fake smile I can muster.

"Since birth," Hawk says, wiggling his eyebrows at me.

I frown at his blatant exaggeration.

"No, seriously." He crosses his finger over his chest. "Tobs... sorry, Tob*ias* and I were actually born on the same day in the *same* hospital. Pretty cool, huh?"

"Wow. That's... weird."

Hawk's eyes twinkle as he leans into me, clearly getting ready to tell a bigger story. "Weird but cool, right? It's like we were destined to be friends."

Tobias groans. "It doesn't hurt that we happen to live right next door to each other either." His eyes are focused on his glass of water, yet not really seeing it at all.

Every time he speaks, his voice vibrates through my skin and into my soul. I ache to hear more of it.

"You don't believe in destiny?" Hawk asks Tobias. "You honestly think it's a coincidence that your mom adopted you and then bought the house right next to mine?"

Tobias looks up at me, catching me off guard. His eyes, like a shot of espresso, shoot through me like an arrow. Those eyes, that see every piece of me but don't flinch at the ugliness I know is there.

"There's no such thing as destiny." Tobias says, looking straight at me. He lowers his eyes, and it leaves me cold. "And Hawk shouldn't believe in it either," he adds with a certain edge to his voice. "Because if it was real, Hawk would have found *her* by now."

Hawk almost growls as he sits up in his seat. His fists are clenched. He's pissed.

"Found who?" I say, trying to calm down the beast that just awakened inside Hawk.

The two of them continue to glare at each other. They are having a battle of the eyes. Even though Hawk is the physically stronger of the two, it's clear that Tobias' glare will win this fight. A moment later, Hawk sighs and lowers his eyes in defeat.

"The *one,*" Tobias says, not taking his eyes off his friend.

"I don't follow."

Hawk rakes his hand through his hair before he speaks. "Tobs here is referring to the girl that was born the same night we were." There is no correction of Tobias' name this time. "He doesn't believe she's the one I'm destined to be with."

I have to stifle a laugh. *Was he for real?* "Um, it's not that uncommon for three babies to be born on the same night... " His eyes pinch together as though I have hurt him, and I instantly regret saying anything.

"Well, maybe where you're from, but here in Webster, multiple births don't happen that often."

The way he said 'where you're from,' like I'm sort of a second class citizen, gets under my skin. "Where I'm from?" I question, batting my eyelashes. "I happen to be from Webster myself." *Asshole.*

"I thought you said you just moved here," Tobias says.

"I just moved back," I say, smiling at Hawk. "I was born here. We didn't stay long." My voice drops off at the sudden pain that memory brings.

Hawk shares a glance with Tobias. "When were you born?" He asks, softly.

"October 14th."

"What year?" Tobias speaks this time. His skin has grown a bit pale. It makes me uneasy.

"2011. Why?"

Hawk cocks his head looking at me. Disbelief seeps into his face. "Tell me your name."

There is something unnerving about the way he asks, so I tell him. "It's Jada."

"Jada Jeanne Williams?" Hawk asks, slowly-- carefully.

My skin turns pale.

"How did you--I've never told anyone my middle name before." It was *her* name. A name I've forced myself to forget. "How did you know my name?" I push away from him in the booth until my back is touching the wall.

Hawk turns to look at me. "It's you." The reverence with which he says that makes me shiver.

"It's me what?" I ask, afraid to know the

answer.

Tobias pushes out of the booth and glares at me. "You're the girl. The one he's *destined* to be with."

I blink at him, stung by his sudden hostility.

Before I can form a thought, Tobias is halfway out of the restaurant.

My body aches to follow him, but Hawk is blocking my way, inching closer to me. His face is filled with wonder.

"I can't believe I found you." He brushes the back of his hand against my cheek. His touch sends a deep chill down my spine.

Chapter 4

Tobias

Damn it! Just... damn it! My fists fly through the air in frustration. *Why? Why does Hawk get everything he ever wants? It just isn't fair!*

I've never asked for anything. I've never even complained about being born with a lung that is going to kill me, never wished my birth parents didn't abandon me. I've never held a grudge with God, until now. Right now, I'm pissed; pissed that He is doing this to me. Why does He have to show me that someone like her exists, if He is just going to give her to Hawk?

It's just downright cruel.

I start pacing in front of the restaurant. The morning air is trying its best to cool my temper down. I'm so angry that all I want to do is go back there and claim what's rightfully mine.

Gah, listen to me! 'Claim what's rightfully mine?' What is wrong with me? I'm acting like a complete Neanderthal around her.

This isn't like me. I need to calm down. All I need to do is get away from her, then I'll be fine.

My eyes dart around me to find a place to go. The first place I see is the woods up ahead. That will be perfect.

Space. You just need some space to think and chill out. Then I'll be fine.

Looking back one last time at the restaurant, I duck into the woods, trying to ignore the mounting pressure that's building inside me with each step I take away from her. Annoyed, I will my feet to push harder against the earth and deeper into the woods.

The extra exertion I'm forcing on my body is, of course, affecting my lungs. I curse, stopping to dig out my inhaler. I hate being so damn weak! I can't even get upset like a normal person!

Screw it. I'm not using my inhaler yet. I can go more than a few yards without that damn crutch! Ignoring the burning feeling inside my lungs, I push farther up a steep incline. I'll take a puff when I get to the top. I can make it to the top of one stupid hill.

When I'm a few feet away from the top, I realize how wrong I am. Dumbo has returned, and he's brought a few friends. *Shit.*

Crushing pressure starts to squeeze my lungs shut, almost dropping me to my knees. My fingers fumble to get a better hold on my inhaler. They shake as I try to get the cap off. I try to steady them, but my palms have now gotten all sweaty. Before I can stop it from happening, the inhaler slides out of my grasp and tumbles down the hill. I stare, dumfounded as it buries itself somewhere in the fallen leaves below. Wheezing, I sink to my knees.

I am now officially screwed. I didn't think to

grab my e-port before I left the restaurant. No one knows I'm out here and there's no way in hell I'm making it back down that hill before I run out of oxygen.

Collapsing onto the ground, I do the only thing I can do. I try to calm down and slow my breathing, because if I don't, I may need to start saying my goodbyes to the world.

Jada

Now that Tobias has left, Hawk won't stop looking at me. It's freaking me out. He doesn't even seem to care that his friend just bolted out the door.

"I can't believe you're really here," Hawk whispers. There is such wonder in his voice that it makes me swallow hard. "I've been looking for you since I was twelve. Honest to God. Did you know we were dubbed the 'Circle of Life Babies'?" His eyes are bright, eager to please me.

"Um, no." My lips pinch together, confused. Hawk shifts closer to me.

"Yeah, because the night we were born three teenagers died in the ER on the floor just below us. Tobias' mom worked in the nursery back then. That's how I know all about you. They say that we're proof that life goes on." He gives me a kind smile. The sort of smile that should make a girl turn to putty except it doesn't work on me. It's not his fault. I'm simply flawed when it comes to all things lovey-dovey.

"Weird," I blurt out, unsure what he wants me to say. I realize at once that's not what he wanted to hear, but I'm getting antsy. I want to leave. I have an overwhelming need to make sure Tobias is all right.

"Hey, are you sure your friend is okay?" I can't help myself. It slipped out.

Hawk's smile fades. "Tobs? Yeah, he's fine. Why wouldn't he be?"

My stomach rolls, suddenly. Worry prickles my brow. Something is wrong. I can feel it.

"He just looked a little pale when he left, that's all."

"Oh, that." He looks over his shoulder as though making sure no one will overhear what he's about to say. "He'd probably kill me for telling you this. He hates it when people think he's weak." I know the feeling. "The dude's got asthma."

I cover my mouth in shock. These days Asthma is practically a death sentence. Pollution levels got too high for medicine to keep up, so most people with asthma die before they hit thirty.

As though sensing my concern, Hawk continues. "He's had it since he was a kid, but his mom is a nurse, so she got him in to see the best docs and stuff. He's got a bad lung too, which makes it even harder. That's actually why he was adopted. His folks couldn't handle having a sick kid."

My eyes bulge, suddenly anxious.

Hawk grabs my hand and cradles it in his. Like a fool, I don't refuse it. I'm surprised by how cold it feels around mine. "He's fine, Jada. He just...has to be careful."

"Careful? How?" I probably shouldn't be

asking these questions since it's really none of my business, but I can't stop myself.

"I don't know... little things. Like being aware of his surroundings. He says he has a hard time in big crowds, not enough air or something. The smog kills him too, of course. He's got this inhaler he has to use, like, all the time." Hawk rubs his thumb against my hand and still I don't pull away. I'm too stunned to move. "Bit of advice. If you wanna be friends with Tobias, you should probably learn CPR." He laughs softly. "I've had to breathe life back into that boy more times then I care to admit."

"It's that bad?" My voice comes out in a whisper.

"Yeah, but don't worry," he says, leaning in so close that I can smell the coffee on his breath. "He's got soft lips." He gives me a quick wink and instantly I'm blushing at the errant thought of Tobias' lips.

Hawk nudges my shoulder bringing me out of my daydream. "He's a tough kid. He'll be okay."

No. He won't. Something is wrong. I just know it. I need to find Tobias. I need to find him—now. But first, I have to get past Hawk.

"Um, I need to use the rest room," I lie. I'm not exactly sure why I didn't just tell him I wanted to leave. There is something about the look he's giving me tells me he wouldn't let me leave without a fight. I don't have time for that.

He looks at me suspiciously but then slides out of the booth to let me out.

"Be right back," I assure him. I walk to the front of the restaurant and can feel his eyes on me. I push my way into the ladies room and wait for a minute before risking a peek through the door. Hawk is talking to the waiter, so I take the opportunity to bolt out of the restaurant. Just like Tobias had.

Once I'm outside my eyes search the streets, but I know in my gut that's not where he is. *Where did you go?*

A crow shrieks in the woods beside me and I blink. The woods. He's there. I know it. I can *feel* him pulling me towards him. I don't have to tell my feet where to go. They drag me along, urging me to go faster.

As soon as the woods envelop me, I know I'm right. My skin is prickling in anticipation. I stop every few feet looking and listening for some clue but all that surrounds me is death: rotting trees and decaying leaves. Even the birds have stopped singing. Panic fills me. *Am I too late?*

As I start to climb a steep incline, I hear something so soft, I swear I imagined it. I stop and listen again. It's a small, faint whistling sound. No, not whistling--wheezing.

"Tobias!" I shout. I only hear my voice echo back.

I shout again, knowing I heard something. I hold my breath and listen with every fiber of my body. *Where are you?*

"Help," a voice whispers so faint that it could have easily been mistaken for the breeze.

But it's not the wind. It's Tobias. And he's hurt.

As fast as I can, I climb the steep hill. I stop short when I reach the top. There he is, on his back, white as a ghost, clutching his sides and gasping for breath. He is going to die. I can see it in the pale blue coloring creeping into his face.

"You're going to be okay," I say automatically, kneeling down beside him. He gives me a weak nod.

His lips part as he tries to speak, so I lower my head to hear him.

"Need...inhaler...fell down... hill," he gasps.

"Right. On it." Turning, I start back down the same cursed hill I'd just worked my way up!

In my hurry to get down the hill, I don't watch where I step, slip on some leaves and end up falling flat on my ass. Blood trickles down my arm from where a rock punctured me during my landing. Ignoring the pain, I start frantically searching the ground for the inhaler. The only problem is that I have no idea what it looks like, and I am running out of time.

I'm about to scream in frustration when I spot something bright yellow a few yards away, half buried under a fallen leaf. His inhaler. *Thank you*, I whisper to the heavens.

Bending over to pick it up, blood runs down my arm at a good clip. *Damn!* I've cut myself pretty good. Seeing my blood drop to the ground actually makes me feel light headed, especially after what I lost this morning. I have to stop this bleeding if I'm going to be of any use to Tobias. Cursing at myself for not wearing anything even remotely usable as a tourniquet, I rip my tank off (leaving me in just my bra) and tie it as tight as I can around my arm. It's not pretty but it'll have to do. Tobias is waiting.

Heading back up the hill I yell, "I've got it!" *Don't die.*

I stumble a few times on my way back, but I

manage to keep a death grip on the inhaler. When I reach the top, Tobias is on his side and barely breathing. I sink down to my knees beside him.

"Here!" I shove the plastic opening against his lips, but he turns his head away from me slightly.

"Cover," he whispers.

I glance down at my chest. Is he really asking me to cover myself up now? I shake my head frustrated with him and push the medicine back at his face.

"Cap...on," he tries again.

Huh? Oh, the cap! Idiot! The cover is still on the inhaler!

Ripping it away, I lift his head up onto my knees and place the plastic once again to his lips. I squeeze down on the depressor as he inhales weakly. Nothing happens.

"Again?"

His eyes blink: *Yes.*

I press it again and hold my breath. This time his chest rises but only a bit. Without waiting for consent, I press it again.

That's when he starts coughing. Coughing is good, right? If he can cough, he can breathe. At least that's what I hope it means.

Though he seems stronger, I give him yet another pump of the medicine. He holds his hand up after he takes it in and then closes his eyes. For a moment, I panic, thinking he's dead, but when he opens his eyes again I exhale in relief. His color is returning. I can see it even through the sheen of sweat covering his face.

He's only still for a moment before the coughing gets worse. He tries to push himself up.

I do my best to sit him upright until he's leaning up against my chest. After a few good coughs, he seems to be able to take steadier breaths although he is still clearly very weak.

"Lie back down," I order. He does. I'm guessing he only complies because he's too exhausted to object.

"Thank you," Tobias croaks, once he's nestled safely back in my lap.

"Shh. Don't talk. Just breathe."

"Good plan."

He closes his eyes and takes some shallow breaths that slowly, very slowly, become deeper. A few brief coughing rounds follow. Each time a cough rolls through his body, I can't help but run my fingers through his dark, curly hair, trying to soothe him. His head is just sitting there, resting in my lap. What else am I supposed to do?

"That feels nice," he says, when the coughing finally subsides. There is the faintest hint of a smile on his lips, so of course I stop. I'm majorly embarrassed.

"Are you okay?" I ask, my voice desperate for the truth.

"I'm right as rain."

"I'm being serious here. Do we need to get you to the hospital? Do you need CPR?" I know I am being annoying with the twenty questions, but I don't know what else to do.

He holds up his inhaler and waves it in the air.

"I'm okay. Thanks to this and you," he says slowly. He starts to sit up again. I inch backwards, making room for him. "Man, I thought I was a goner there for a minute." Rubbing the back of his neck, he catches sight of my arm. My hand instantly reaches to make sure my cuff hasn't slipped revealing my ugly truth. That's not the arm he's looking at though. He's looking at my other arm. The bloody one. And... my bra. *Whoops!*

I blush ten shades of ruby and quickly cover myself with my hands. His eyes widen when he looks at my tourniquet, not my chest. Something flashes across his eyes. He's angry. He pushes up to his feet but wobbles a bit as he does. "What happened to your arm?"

"It's nothing," I say, standing up to meet him, grabbing his arm to steady him. "I scratched it trying to get your inhaler." I wince at the memory. "I'm not the most graceful person in the world."

He frowns and then starts shrugging himself out of his t-shirt.

"Um, what are you doing?" I ask, trying my best not to look at his naked chest. I'm not doing a very good job of it.

"I'm giving you my shirt," he says.

"Oh. Yeah. Good idea." Mortified at my own stupidity, I pull his shirt over my head and then hug my arms around my waist. His scent envelops me and I can't help but breathe him in. It's downright intoxicating. He smells like...home. Whatever that is.

I accidentally slip another peek at his body as he sits down on a rock. Although he's not built like Hawk, he's not as scrawny as you'd think. He's a lover, not a fighter. I bite my lip to hold back the burning in my cheeks.

I shuffle my feet on the ground, not sure how long my legs will let me be this far away from him.

When I look up at him, he's staring at me, his eyebrows wrinkling in concentration.

"How did you know I was here?" he asks.

It's a legitimate question but one I don't have a rational answer for.

"I don't know." The truth spills out. "I just sort of...knew."

His face is surprised at first but then becomes contorted, almost as though he's in pain again.

"What is it? What's wrong?" I ask taking a step towards him.

He looks beyond me to the edge of the hill. "We have company," he says, nostrils flaring.

I don't have time to process his answer before I hear what he's talking about.

"Tobs? Where are you man?"

It's Hawk. His footsteps are swift along the dirt as he climbs the hill. Tobias gets up and takes a step in front of me, as though he's trying to protect me and I don't stop him. I'm a little scared of Hawk's reaction at finding me here, too.

As he crests the hill, Hawk's face goes from relieved at seeing his friend alive to what I can only describe as instant fury. I'm surprised at how deeply his glare cuts me.

"What's going on?" Hawk asks Tobias. "What's she doing here? And why don't you have a shirt on?" His voice is laced with accusation. I don't like that. Not one bit.

I step away from Tobias and stand directly in between them before Tobias can stop me. "He had an asthma attack. I helped him." My words are not eloquent but the way he glares at me...it makes me nervous.

Hawk's eyes narrow as he crosses his thick arms over his chest. I do my best not to let my eyes linger on the way his shirt clings to his pecs, because I know that's what he wants. Still, it's hard to avoid. He looks right at me when he speaks again.

"You were supposed to be in the bathroom."

Busted. I swallow. Here goes nothing. "Look, you freaked me out back there with your 'Circle of Life' stuff. I just needed some air. That's all. When I walked outside I heard Tobias yelling for help."

I glance to Tobias hoping he'll go along with my version of the truth.

"It's true, man," Tobias says. "If it hadn't been for her I'd be halfway to heaven by now."

Hawk's eyes narrow again before he exhales. He seems to buy our story. "Okay, that explains you. But why were you out in the woods, Tobs?"

I'm curious to know the answer to that myself.

Tobias steps away from us, as though embarrassed. "The air was getting too thick in there."

"So, you walked to the middle of the woods, where no one could find you, for air?" he asks, clearly pissed.

"You found me," Tobias retorts.

Hawk snorts. "That's only because you stink."

I look at Hawk, offended for Tobias.

"What he means is that he can track my scent," Tobias tells me. "I don't stink," he spits at Hawk.

I'm confused. "What does that mean, you can track him?"

A small smile spreads across Hawk's face. "What can I say? I've got a good nose."

"Okay, now that is creepy," I say.

He sniffs the air again. "Who is bleeding?"

Tobias shoves a thumb at me. "She scratched her arm trying to get my inhaler. That's why I took off my shirt. She used her own shirt as a tourniquet to try and stop the bleeding."

"You're hurt?" Hawk's eyes shift.

I grab my arm. "I'm fine, really."

"Let me look," he says.

"No, it's fine."

His eyes shift to my other arm. To my leather cuff. My eyes follow what he sees: a small trail of blood has escaped its prison. I must have re-opened the 'J' when I fell. Panicked, my eyes find his. Pleading. He gives me a small nod before he starts to undo the bandage around my other arm.

Blood has soaked through the tank I'd used to try and stop the bleeding and is now caked all over my arm.

Hawk frowns, then lifts his shirt up and starts to undo his belt.

I flinch back from him and I don't know why.

"What are you doing?" Tobias asks, stepping forward. Hawk pulls off his belt with a loud crack and I jump at the sound.

"The shirt isn't cutting it. Her blood isn't clotting." He pushes Tobias aside, pulls out a knife from his back pocked and carves a small hole a few inches away from the buckle. He orders me to sit, which I do, then wraps the leather around my arm and pulls the belt closed. The blood slows down almost immediately.

"Better," Hawk says, before he takes off his

shirt to sop up the mess left behind.

I gulp as I glance secretly back and forth between the two of them. I'm sitting in the middle of the woods with two half-naked men. Not a bad way to start the day.

Chapter 5

Tobias

The walk back home is, by far, one of the hardest things I've ever had to do. Not because I don't feel well, but because I actually feel pretty damn good, considering. It sucks because Hawk gets to hold onto Jada's waist the whole way home. He claims he needs to hang onto her in case she gets lightheaded from the blood loss. She tries to protest, but nobody wins a fight with Hawk.

When we drop her off at her house, Hawk makes her promise to see a doctor about her cut. The look she gives me tells me she has no intention of doing that, but she agrees anyway.

Now that it's just the two of us, Hawk can't seem to wipe that stupid grin off his face.

"What are you so giddy about?" I ask, rubbing my chest. It's starting to get tight again. My medicine must be wearing off.

Hawk stops walking and looks at me. "Are you serious? You don't know why I'm so happy? I found her, man! I found her!"

"Yeah, that's pretty wild," I croak, trying not to sound like the wind has just been knocked out of me.

"It's not wild. It's fate. I was meant to find her."

I can't help but get mad. "Why? Just because you share the same birthday?"

He looks at me, shocked. "Not just the same birthday, Tobs, the same hospital. Can't you see that it's fate?"

"Fate, huh? I was born that day too, in case you forgot. In that same hospital. Why is it that you get to have a fate of being with her while I get stuck with the fate of dying?" I hiss, unaware of how angry I really am.

"Wow," he whispers. "I didn't know you felt that way about her."

"This isn't about her," I lie. "It's about how you're *always* getting what you want. Always. It just—pisses me off sometimes."

Shaking, I start walking again, trying to calm down. I can't believe I just said that out loud. Although I may have secretly thought it for years, I never dreamed I'd actually have the balls to say it. Now that it's out, there is no way to take it back. He'll probably never forgive me. Not that I'd blame him. That was a pretty shitty thing to say.

I only manage a few yards before he catches up to me and steps in front of me, forcing me to a stop again. His eyes are pinched tight.

"You're pissed at *me* because *I* get everything?" he asks. "You have got to be kidding me!" His face is red and his lips are drawn into a tight line. "You're the one who has everything."

Of all the things I thought he might say, that

wasn't one of them.

"What do I have, Hawk, that you could possibly want? Asthma? You can have it. Or would you rather have the diseased lung that's going to kill me one day? Take it! It's all yours!" I shout.

He turns away from me and his shoulders slump. No. I didn't think so. No one would want that.

"At least you have someone who actually cares about you," Hawk says. "I'd give anything to have a mom like yours."

Um, that came out of left field. Although it was true that he and his folks don't have the closest relationship, I didn't think it could really be that bad. I mean, they are rich, at least compared to us. He's never wanted for anything. How could he ever be jealous of me?

"Hawk, what are you talking about? Your parents care about you." At least I assume they do. He always hung out at my house, but that was only because they work all the time. Right?

He laughs quietly and kicks a rock into the ditch. "They care if I make quarterback or get a scholarship, but they don't care a damn for me."

"You're over exaggerating," I say, hoping I'm right.

He shakes his head.

"I'm not."

His voice is sadder than I've ever heard it before. It makes me stop and realize how little I know about him. What a huge chunk of his life he's chosen to keep to himself. I always just assumed he had nothing to complain about, but looking at him now, I wonder how much he's held back.

"Sometimes I get so angry, you know?" he says, looking out into the woods. "It's like, this rage comes from out of nowhere. I don't know what to do with it, so I take it out on them, I guess. I don't know. We yell a lot at my place. They don't get me. I guess that's part of the reason why I like to hunt. It seems to calm me down somehow." He pulls his hair in frustration. "I sound like a crazy man, huh?"

I don't want to admit that he does sound a bit out there, but I can sense that edge to him. He has some anger issues sure, but it's just hormones. He's just got a lot of them.

"Sounds like pretty normal stuff to me," I lie.

"Let me ask you something," Hawk says. "What do I want to do when I graduate?"

That's easy. Anyone who knows Hawk knows what he wants to do with his life.

"Hunt," I say.

He nods. "So how come you know what I love and my folks don't, huh?" He runs his hands through his hair, pulling at the roots. "God, can you even imagine if they ever found out that I was hunting those turkeys?" He gives a weak laugh. "They'd probably call the cops themselves just to be rid of me."

I want to tell him he's wrong, but something in the way he hangs his head makes me think he might be right. That's the sort of posture one has to earn.

When finally he looks up at me his expression is tired. "That's why finding Jada..." he says to the sky, "is so important. I feel--calmer with her. I know I just met her, but it feels like she belongs with me. And..." He pauses. He wants to say something, but he's struggling to get the words out, so I wait. "I *have* to believe that there is someone in this world who is meant for me. To love *me*." His last sentence is so low that I don't really think he meant to say it out loud.

And right there in the street, seeing Hawk look more broken than I have ever seen him before, I let my feelings for Jada go. What sort of friend would I be if I didn't?

Jada

When I get home, the first thing I do is jump in the shower. My hands are covered with mud and blood from my gash. The soap stings like a son-of-a-bitch, but I can't risk it getting infected. Infections mean hospitals, and hospitals aren't the type to over look a girl who carves her name into her own flesh. They'll ship me off to the loony bin for sure; hence the soap.

I will have to think of something to tell Hawk when he asks about what I'm hiding, but there will be time to think of an excuse later. Right now, I just need to take care of my latest scar.

After my shower, I dump out a healthy dose of liquid band-aid to seal the gash and change into some old yoga pants and a long sleeve shirt to try and mask the mess that is my arm.

I head downstairs to see if Dad's home yet. Noticing that the coast is still clear, I run back up the stairs and into his bedroom. I know just the thing that will take away not only the pain but the memory as well: Dad's anti-anxiety tabs. He's been on them for years. They are a blessing and a curse. On the one hand, it keeps him from being so damn sad. But on the other, if he is on them when he drinks, he'll forget his cruelness. Experience has taught me it's better to find yourself out of the reach of his right hook when he pops one of these babies.

Of course, that also means he forgets where he puts the damn pills, so I always have to hunt for them whenever I need one. I don't dare take more than a few at a time in case he does remember how many he had. Even the pills wouldn't blur the memory of that punishment.

After looking through all the usual spots, I find them tucked safely inside an envelope behind his dresser. He's getting crafty.

I'm about to slip a few in my bag when I hear him come in downstairs. Panicking, I shove the whole bottle inside and race down the stairs, doing my best to look casual.

"Get dressed," Dad grunts when I walk into the kitchen.

"I am dressed." I blink at him, annoyed.

He looks at me but doesn't really see me. "Ms. Philips invited us over for dinner tonight to thank me for fixing her water heater."

I groan. I don't want to eat dinner at some strange woman's house.

"We need to be there in an hour. Wake me up. I'm taking a nap," he says, before he heads upstairs. He takes a 'nap' everyday. Of course, he doesn't actually sleep. He holds vigil for her.

For years, I actually believed that he was sleeping, until one day I was playing downstairs and I thought I heard him sobbing. Worried, I ran to his room to make sure he was okay.

It was the one and only time he had neglected to shut the door all the way. Through the crack, I saw my father on his knees, weeping. Above him was a mini shrine to Mom. There was a photo of her on what looked like their wedding day and a candle burning softly beside it. In his hands, he grasped a rosary.

It wasn't seeing my father so upset that changed me. I saw that everyday. It was what he said that day that scarred me forever. He said out loud, for his wonderful and precious God to hear, that he wished I'd never been born.

I was seven.

My mother was dead and my father had just forsaken me.

On that day, there was a definite shift inside me. A closing of doors. A hardening of the heart. I learned in one day how toxic love really was. It didn't help that it was also the day he started taking the pills and the fun really began.

I started cutting shortly after that. I think it was because he always called me my mother's name, Jeanne, when he hit me. I started etching my name into my skin to remind me I wasn't her. Sometimes it worked. Sometimes it didn't. On those darker days, I had to remind myself that I was made out of titanium. He couldn't hurt me no matter what he did. No one could. Over the years I've closed myself off so much. There is *no* chance in hell anyone is getting in here. Not anymore. My heart is dead-bolted behind a wall of titanium now.

Outside a rumble of thunder booms in the distance. I glance out the window. The sky has taken on a greenish glow. It's actually scary. Guess they weren't lying about storms coming. The electricity surging outside is almost palpable.

The ominous clouds bring with them a marked shift in the temperature as well. The humidity is starting to roll in. Groaning, I head back upstairs and dig around in my room for something that isn't so damn hot but will also cover my new scar. All I can find is my dark gray knit lace-up summer sweater that I used to wear all the time when we lived in Phoenix. When I pair it with a black tank, it actually manages to hide my marks and look somewhat intentional. The way the sweater falls off my shoulder makes the fact that it's way too big, look hip. Even the cut-off jeans, which I used when I painted my room, looked suitable. The globs of black paint covering them look neat. Not exactly my Sunday best but it will have to do. My wardrobe isn't exactly compatible with these sudden shifts in temperature. All the other cities we've lived in never had this level of humidity. It doesn't make sense. We live in New Hampshire. Why is it so damn hot?

At six o'clock, Dad and I make our way over to Ms. Philips' house in silence. We walk across our connecting yards, stepping on the overgrown grass on her side. The paint on her trailer is chipping in several spots, and some of the windows have duct tape along the edges. It looks like our house isn't the only one on the block in need of some serious TLC.

Planting on a smile, Dad knocks on her door.

This is going to suck.

When Ms. Philips opens the door, however,

my heart stops.

My limp smile turns into a real one, but I have no idea why. Looking at her feels like finding a long lost friend. *Kari!* A voice in my head shouts. I blink at how strongly the name comes across. The only problem is that I don't know anyone named Kari.

Aside from being uber-familiar, she's also gorgeous. Ms. Philips is gorgeous! She's old, like my dad, but still has an undeniable beauty. She's tall and lean, like a dancer, with eyes that are sad, but still manage to sparkle. I glance at Dad, who has gone a little red in the cheeks. No wonder he spent all day fixing her water heater.

"So good to meet you, Jada," Ms. Philips says, holding out her hand.

"You too, Ms. Philips."

"Please, call me Kari. Ms. Philips makes me sound old!" She smiles.

My eyes widen. *How did I know her name was Kari?*

Dad must have said her name before. That has to be it.

"I don't know what I would have done if your Dad hadn't offered to help me," Kari continues, ushering us into her living room. She gestures toward her fake leather couch for us to sit. My thighs squeak against the material.

Her place is smaller than ours, but vastly more homey. She has handmade blankets lining all the edges of the chairs in her tiny living room, which makes sense. A place like this probably gets pretty cold at night. Even though everything in her house looks worn, it's like someone actually lives here. Our places always look like we're ready to move.

Running my fingers over her pleather couch, I can actually see myself living here, ratty carpet and all.

Behind the couch there is an entire wall dedicated to picture frames. It's wild. We don't have a single one up in our place. Not even a digital one. Pictures evoke memories and memories are banned at our house, especially ones of my mother.

"Thanks again for inviting us over," Dad says, clearly uncomfortable.

"It's my pleasure. It's not often I get to cook for someone."

She's pretty and she cooks. Interesting.

"So Jada, will you be starting school Monday?"

I nod. "Yup. Senior year. And before you ask, I'm not going to college." That's always the follow-up question. Might as well nip that conversation in the bud. I brace myself for the adult lecture about college being essential, but she surprises me.

"I wish I'd never gone. College proved to be hell for me," Kari says. I can't help but notice that her eyes have teared up. "Will you excuse me," she says, after a moment. "I need to check on the roast."

As she tinkers in the kitchen, I get up and walk over to her wall of frames, curious to know more about our lovely neighbor. There are the traditional family style portraits of Kari as a child. She was stunning even from early on. Then there are some of her in her teens dressed in a purple leotard and rainbow leg warmers. I knew it. She was a dancer.

It's the photo just over the couch that pulls my focus though. I hone in on one black and white still. It's a shot of two dancers: a man and woman. The woman isn't Kari, though. This dancer has super pale skin with jet black hair; the contrast is simply amazing. She's reaching out one of her hands towards the other dancer. He's the stark opposite of her. His skin is dark and he has black curly hair. His face is terribly scarred--but it doesn't, ironically, deter from his overt beauty.

My heart races. *I know these people.* How do I know these people?

Breathing heavily, I look at the picture of the two of them reaching out to each other. There is a deep and palpable longing in their eyes that I've never seen captured on film before. It's beautiful and heartbreaking at the same time. I can't pull myself away from it. It's like her pain is my pain, and achingly familiar.

"That's from a production of *Romeo & Juliet,*" Kari says, from right beside me, scaring the daylights out of me.

"Oh," I say, trying to find my heart again. "That's the one where they die, right?"

Her face drops. "Yeah. That's the one." She blinks a few times, almost as if she's fighting back tears. "Dinner is ready." She turns and walks back into the kitchen.

There's a story there. I need to find out what it is. I just don't know why.

Chapter 6

Tobias

When we get home, Hawk's folks aren't there yet, so I invite him over to help me make lunch since we never actually got to eat earlier. He grabs clean t-shirts off the clothes line before we head inside. We have a dryer, but my mom is so old school that she refuses to use it when its sunny out.

Since Mom is still sleeping, we busy ourselves in the kitchen. Hawk pours himself a glass of powdered milk while I look through the pantry for our options. I opt for something simple, spaghetti and frozen meatballs. Hawk fries up the meatballs while I boil the water.

Neither one of us mentions the strange silence that's managed to wedge its way between us.

"I can't stay long," Hawk finally says. "I've got practice at 2:30."

I nod. He's been going to football practice for the last month now, leaving me to twiddle my thumbs in boredom. Today, I think I might welcome his absence.

"How's that going?"

He taps the spatula on the edge of the pan. "I'd rather be out in the woods."

"One more year, dude, then you'll be free." It's a weak reply but it's all I can come up with.

Hawk smiles. "And won't the folks be happy when I tell them what they can do with their college fund?"

I have always known that college was out of the picture for me with my limited time left on this planet, but have assumed Hawk would go until now.

"No college, huh? What's the plan then? Sit around and wait for me to die?" I say, only half-kidding.

He laughs. "As much fun as that will be, I guess my plans are dependent on what Jada wants to do." He turns the heat off the stove and drains the fat as I stand there and stare at him in disbelief.

"What are you talking about?"

He brushes past me, grabs a pot hanging from the rack and tosses the browned meatballs in.

"My plans are contingent on hers." He stirs in a jar of sauce.

"Hawk," I say, carefully. "You just met her."

He looks me in the eyes. "And now that I found her I'm not going to lose her." Something shifts in his expression. His jaw is set, determined. For a second he looks downright dangerous. Then it shifts back and he looks like himself again.

Mom starts to come down the stairs just

then. I glance at the clock and notice that she hasn't slept enough.

"Hawk, sugar," Mom says, rubbing her eyes. "You staying for lunch?" She asks.

"If you'll have me," he beams. Hawk adores my mom and she feels the same for him. It's hard for me to grasp that Hawk doesn't get this at home. I wonder, suddenly, what that sort of cold shoulder might do to a person.

As we eat, Hawk talks my mom's ear off about everything except Jada, for which I'm grateful, but I can't help but wonder why. Maybe he wants to keep her all to himself. When he tells her about my asthma attack, though, I want to haul off and punch him.

"Tobias Daniel Garret," Mom growls. "You march your asthmatic little butt up those stairs and put your nebulizer on this minute!" I glare at Hawk who gives me an 'I'm sorry' look.

"Ma, I'm fine."

She crosses her arms and cocks her head. "Now, mister."

I grumble. There's no getting out of it once she's gone all protective mama-hen on me. "Thanks a lot, Hawk," I say, tossing my napkin down.

"Anytime, bro." He gives me his sweet and innocent smile. I know he's only trying to help, but I hate being treated like a baby.

As I climb the stairs, I hear Hawk offering to help my mom clean up the dishes.

A dark thought worms its way into my head. When I'm dead, Hawk will be there, waiting to take over my role as Mom's son.

In the end, Hawk *will* get everything he

wants.

Jada

I eat the roast in silence as Kari and Dad talk about the plumbing work she needs done in her bathroom. It's a riveting conversation.

"Shouldn't take more than a couple of days," Dad says, forking a carrot into his mouth.

Kari seems to follow along in the conversation but keeps looking at me funny.

"I'm sorry I keep staring, Jada," Kari says. "It's just—you remind me so much of a friend of mine and I can't figure out why. You don't look anything like her except that she was about your age when she died."

I swallow my piece of beef. "Oh, wow. Um, I'm sorry?" It comes out more as a question than a genuine concern for her friend. I'm an ass. "What was her name?" I say, trying to cover my sensitivity.

"Naya. Almost the same as yours."

Naya. There's that name again. Sweat beads against my forehead.

"Um, can I use your bathroom?" I hear myself ask, needing to get some air.

Kari gives me a funny look before she points me to the room just past the living room. I scoot out from the table and dash towards the restroom only to come face to face with that damn picture again.

Those eyes...*why are they so familiar?* Without meaning to, my fingers reach up and remove the photo from the wall. They trace along the edge of the boy's scarred face with such longing and passion that they actually start to shake.

"Who are you?" I whisper to the photo.

"Those were my friends, Naya and Etash." Kari's voice whispers.

I nearly jump out of my skin.

"Sorry. Didn't mean to scare you. I just forgot to tell you to wiggle the handle on the flush when you're done."

The flush. Right. I'm supposed to be peeing. My fingers fumble to put the picture back but they've grown all sweaty now and, before I can stop it, the frame slips out of my fingers and shatters to bits at my feet. I gasp as though the glass pierced me instead of her carpet.

"I'm so sorry," I say, quickly bending down to clean up the shards. As I do, however, my bag slips off the couch dumping the contents onto the floor amongst the glass. Dad's tab bottle lands right at her feet. *Shit!*

As fast as I can, I reach out to grab it, but Kari scoops the bottle up first. Her eyes grow dark as she reads the label.

"Why do you have these?" She asks in a low hiss so my dad won't hear.

Snatching them out of her hand, I stand up. "That's none of your business."

She stands in front of me, no doubt judging me. Let her. This has nothing to do with her.

"Hey, Ted, can you come in here a minute?" Kari calls to my dad, keeping her eyes planted on me.

My eyes grow wide. *She wouldn't. Would she?*

Dad walks into the living room still chewing

his food. Kari doesn't bat an eye when he stands beside her. If she's waiting for me to confess, she's wasting her time. I clench my jaw to prove my point.

"What's going on?" Dad asks, when no one speaks. He glares at me.

Kari clears her throat. "We had a bit of an accident. Would you mind grabbing the broom from the closet in the kitchen?"

"What did you do?" Dad growls, spinning to face me.

"It was my fault." Kari laughs. "I'm not as graceful as I used to be."

Dad grunts his disbelief but goes to get the broom anyway. I want to thank her for covering for me, but I can't look her in the eye. I'm suddenly too ashamed.

After the glass is cleaned up, Dad uses the lull in conversation to say we should get going.

Kari insists on making us take some of the leftovers home, which I am grateful for. He won't eat it, but I will. It's better than the stale cheese we have waiting at home.

Once we get back into the safety of our place, Dad heads straight to his room and closes the door. Paying his penance for talking to another woman, I suppose.

I sigh.

He'll be in there the rest of the night grieving. Hearing him moan again is something I can't take right now. So I do what I do best. I leave.

In every town we've lived in, the first thing I did was find a place to go when Dad was in one of his moods. So far I have yet to find a place I could use as my escape from him when he 'naps.' I'm starting to loose hope that I'll find one. It makes me think that it's further proof that we're not meant to be here.

Outside on the road, I kick at the rocks filling the potholes, each kick symbolically pushing back some crumb of injustice life has dealt me.

Poor, poor pitiful me.

God, I am pathetic. I want to punch myself I'm so obnoxious.

As I walk beside the woods, I slow my pace. The tall oaks here remind me of Tobias and the day I saved him in the woods. Tobias and his dark eyes, just like the boy in the photo.

Tears start welling for no good reason. Embarrassed by the tears, I duck off into the woods in case one slips out. Crying is what he does; he's the weak one, not me.

Shivering a bit in the night, I glance up through the trees and find the moon. It looks almost full. It's so large and bright that it illuminates the forest floor with just enough light to see the roots that would otherwise land me on my ass. Taking in my surroundings, I admire the massive trees that loom large all around me. They feel like arms holding me, protecting me from the big, bad world. It feels like...home. I found my hideaway.

To my right there is a large moss-covered boulder that's begging to be leaned against. More than ready to comply, I nestle myself against its cold embrace.

Slipping out Dad's tab bottle, I read the label. One of these will take the edge off. Two will make me giddy. I think it might be time to find out what three will do. Shaking out the tabs, I press them firmly against my tongue and wait for them to work their magic.

Chapter 7

Tobias

Over the hum of my nebulizer, I hear Hawk chatting it up with Mom downstairs. Listening to them through the grate in my floor infuriates me. He's waited until I left to talk about Jada. He must not think I can handle hearing about her. It ticks me off that he's right.

I'd be able to make out what they are saying a lot better if I'd just turn off the stupid machine, but then Mom would hear its silence and come flying up the stairs to yell at me. Instead, I have to resort to crawling under my bed and pressing my ear to the grate.

"I found her, Ms. Garret." Hawk is saying.

"Found who, honey?" Mom asks over the sound of dishes being cleared.

"The woman I'm going to marry."

My jaw clenches hearing the reverence in his voice.

"My, my, my," Mom purrs. "What's her name?"

"Jada." I can practically hear the goofy grin

in his voice before a dish breaks.

"Whoa, Ms. G, you okay?"

My pulse quickens thinking that Ma has been hurt. Instantly, I'm up and trying to push myself out from under the bed when I hear Mom speak again.

"Her name is Jada?"

"Yeah, Jada Jeanne Williams." He sighs her name.

The sound of a chair being dragged across the floor echoes inside the grate, followed by the biggest exhalation I've ever heard from my mother.

"Has Tobias met her?" she asks, or at least, I think that's what she said. It's practically whispered.

"Um, yeah. Of course, he made a rotten impression on her. He had his asthma attack shortly after he met her," Hawk explains. "Why are you so pale, Ms. G? You need some water or something?"

"Just a long day, honey. I'll be fine. Tell me more about this girl."

Without skipping a beat, he begins talking about Jada. But he's not describing her right, which is nothing short of maddening. For starters, her hair isn't blonde. It's honey, like the color of wheat fields when the sun is high in the sky. And it isn't wavy at all. Her hair is like silk, cascading down the nape of her neck to the small dip in her back. Her eyes are more than brown. They are the color of coffee, kissed with cream. He can't even get her complexion right. Tan skin? Has he even been looking at the same girl? Jada's skin is ivory, like the clouds in the sky. But even with all of her natural beauty, I know that she doesn't see herself that way by the subtle way she always rolls her shoulders forward. It's like she's trying to hide herself away inside those dark clothes. She doesn't grasp how stunning she really is.

"Hawk?" My mom sounds timid.

"Yeah, Ms. G?"

"Is everything okay at home? I don't mean to pry, but I can't help but hear you and your folks yelling at each other a lot, and I'm worried about you, honey. You'd tell me if something was wrong, wouldn't you?"

I hold my breath so I don't miss his answer.

"I don't really know," he says quietly. "Lately, I just feel different. Like I'm changing somehow."

"Changing? How so?"

He doesn't answer right away. I can almost see his brow crinkle, like he does when he is thinking.

"It's gonna sound weird but now that I've found Jada, I feel like I'm going to lose her somehow. I'm getting really protective of her. I get angry if anyone even looks at her. It's freaking me out."

Mom gives a low whistle.

"Sounds like you've been bitten by the love bug."

"More like swallowed whole," he says.

More dishes clank around until they eventually say their goodbyes. I scoot out from under the bed and peek out from behind the curtains to watch him leave. I'm careful not to be seen. He waves a final goodbye to Mom then walks up to his porch. He stops just short of going inside though. He looks over his shoulder, presumably to make sure Ma's gone inside, then skips back down the steps and heads into the woods. I shake my head. So much for football practice. I wonder how he'll talk the coach out of calling his folks for missing it, but then Hawk can sweet talk a skunk out of spraying. Everyone adores Hawk. Still, it was pretty stupid of him to risk hunting when my mom was home. I don't care if she has fallen under his spell or not. If she catches him hunting, Mom will rat his ass out faster than Hawk can draw back his string. And that's pretty damn fast.

Succumbing to the need for my medicine, I slip the mask back on. Its healing mist makes my head heavy. Without meaning to, I let exhaustion take over.

When I wake, the sky is dark. Sweat drenches the back of my neck. My gut wrenches. Something is wrong, and it's not with me.

I rip off my mask and race down the hall to check to on Ma. Opening her door, I expect to find her missing or hurt, but she's fast asleep in her bed. A soft snore confirms she's breathing. Seeing her safe and sound should have put me at ease, but I'm still anxious about something. *What though?*

After I check the house to make sure nothing is on fire or anything, I head back in my room but still can't sleep. I pace like a caged animal trying to figure out what is wrong.

That's when the hairs on my arms stands up. That's only happened once before: when Jada was near.

Instantly, I fling my window open and half

expect her to be standing outside, but of course there is only the darkness. My heart sinks. As I start to pull my head back in though, I catch a whiff of lilac.

She is outside.

And close enough for the wind to carry her scent with it.

Without thinking, I push my window open all the way and jump out the second story window, landing softly in the flowerbed below. In the seventeen years I've lived here, I've never attempted such a stupid move, so the fact that I didn't break anything is beyond miraculous.

After standing frozen for a moment, I realize Mom didn't hear me jump out, so I begin tip-toeing down the driveway. Once I pass our fence, I start running, not caring in the least that I'm barefoot, or that I am not supposed to run–ever.

Jada

As I wait for the pills to work and my world to disappear, I lean back against the rock again trying to sap away some of its coolness. *Damn, it's hot tonight!* I wish I could just strip down and let the night air cool me down.

Wait. Why can't I? There's no one here.

Standing, I look into the dark woods, just to make sure. The sweater comes off first, exposing my most recent gash to the darkness. It throbs a bit with the fresh air brushing against it, but it's nothing I can't handle.

A small breeze comes through the trees, making my skin goose-bump. The night air feels so good that I peel off my tank top too. Standing in the dark in just my bra and shorts is so liberating.

Wanting to feel nothing but the night sky on my skin, I kick out of my shorts too. Why not? It's not like the squirrels will tell on me.

Standing in just my underwear, I can't help but feel how glorious the moss is under my feet, deliciously cool. Smiling wide, I spin around like a school girl laughing.

Me.

Laughing.

The spinning, however, starts to make me dizzy. I've stopped turning, yet the woods keep traveling on around me. *Whoa. That's freaky.*

I take a step forward to sit down, but I lose my footing and start to fall backwards. I close my eyes and brace myself for the impact but instead of falling flat on my ass, I'm scooped up by two masculine arms.

"Jada!"

The voice is male and kind. His face is blurry for some bizarre reason.

I try to focus my eyes again, but his head splits itself in two, making it really hard to pick one pair of eyes to look at. Ditching my vision I let my eyes roll back in my head where they seem to want to go, and focus instead on his arms. They are so strong and warm. I sigh and cuddle up against them. He knows my name. That's good enough for me.

"Why are you out here in just your underwear?" he asks. His voice sounds weird, almost like he's talking inside a jar.

"Because it's hot out," I mumble and then

smile. "You're hot, too."

Whoa, did I just say that?

Jar Head brushes his hand against my cheek and tucks my hair back behind my ear. *Man, that feels nice.*

"Are you hurt?"

"I'm right as rain," I say, trying to keep my eyes open so he'll actually believe me, whoever he is.

The way his voice wavers, all worried like, it feels *so...*nice. I start to wonder what those large hands of his would feel like against my hot skin.

I lick my lips, deciding not to wonder anymore. I wrap my hands around his neck, and he does the same, almost as though he wants me.

Me.

A slow burn starts in the pit of my stomach, and I like it. I want more. I grab his shirt and pull him to me.

That's when I can finally make out who is standing in front of me.

It's Hawk.

I stop in mid-kiss, trying to blink his cold eyes away. After a few blinks it works. Suddenly Tobias is in front of me, smiling his delicious half-smile. His luscious curls drip down his forehead. Ignoring the truth that lurks inside my head, I let my imagined blue-eyed Tobias brush his thumb against my cheek, wiping away a tear I didn't even know I had.

My breath catches, seeing desire dance in his eyes. I can see it. I can feel it. He *does* want me. Tobias wants me.

"Kiss me," I whisper, closing my eyes in an effort to still the sudden spinning trees.

A second later my wish is granted. His lips crash against mine as heat pools between my legs. His tongue takes mine hostage, causing me to claw my fingers into his back pulling him closer, needing him to devour me.

He releases my lips, which now feel swollen and sore, and begins to attack my neck with deep kisses. My body arches up, desperate for his touch, any touch. Complying, he works his way down to my breasts.

A tiny voice is yelling at me to stop, to push him away, revolted that Hawk is touching me, but I refuse to listen. Deep down, I know it's him and not Tobias running his hands over my skin, but I can't seem to make myself care. Someone is touching me and that's good enough for me.

I tear at Hawk's shirt until he raises up and removes the barrier for me. The hunger on his face is suddenly terrifying, but I'm too far gone to stop him now.

Foolishly, I try to sit up in order to run my hands over his chest but the trees around me start spinning again. His image has blurred into two separate people, each Hawk hungrier than the other.

I close my eyes and try to come back to reality, but when I try to open them back up, they won't budge. An intense heaviness presses down on me, forcing me down onto the ground. The sharp undergrowth slices open my back. I don't stop kissing him though because each kiss pulls me further away from the world. I let myself slip into the darkness that is calling me. The last thing I feel are his fingertips as they rip off my underwear.

After that, there is nothing. Blessed and beautiful, nothing.

Tobias

Her scent leads me to the woods. I realize I should be out of breath, or at the very least using my inhaler, but I didn't even bring it. It's shocking that I don't seem to need it. My feet fly over the fallen branches and twigs as I race towards her scent. I have to stop a few times to sniff the air, but her smell has become so powerful that I'm almost overtaken by it. She's here, I just have to find her. She needs me. I don't know how I know this, but I do.

Cresting a small hill, I see her lying on the ground.

Alone.

And naked.

"Jada!" Half falling, half sliding, I run down the hill toward her.

She's lying on her back with one leg slightly bent. The smallest of frowns covers her sleeping face.

My God, she is beautiful.

It's only when I sink down to the ground to check for her pulse that I see the marks. Large, dirty handprints cover almost every inch of her body.

"Jada!" I shout again, shaking her, but she only moans softly.

Looking around I see that her clothes are scattered in random piles around her. I grab her shirt and do my best to put it back on her limp body. It's an extremely frustrating job having my hands touch her skin while not allowing them to explore every inch of her like they are begging me to.

But I'm not a monster.

As I pull down her shirt, I smell something besides lilac on her skin. Something that makes my blood boil. The scent of a cologne only one person wears.

Hawk.

Bile forms at the back of my throat.

I'll kill him. I swear to God. I'll end him.

Chapter 8

Jada

The sound of the door shutting downstairs feels like a sledge hammer against my eyeballs.

I groan as I open my eyes. Man, my head is killing me.

Pulling back the covers, I yawn. Something scratches at my neck and when I go down to itch it, I notice it's a tag from my shirt, which is on backwards. *Huh?*

My hand reaches up to cradle my throbbing head and feels something crunchy. I yank it out. It's a leaf. *What the hell?*

I stand up and check myself over in the mirror and gasp at what I see. I look awful. My hair is all tangled with even more bits of leaves woven in. Leaning in, I touch my lips. They hurt. They are red and swollen. As I inventory the rest of my body, I notice a few odd bruises. My whole body aches. I feel like I've been tossed around like a rag doll.

What happened last night? Guess I shouldn't have taken three pills. Damn. It's scary, now that

I think about it. I don't even remember walking home.

On the other hand, I did have some pretty intense dreams about Tobias. I'm actually starting to blush just thinking about them. Dangerous, Jada. Dangerous. I am not going to fall for him. I. Am. Not. I will not end up like a lovesick fool like Dad.

I slump my shoulders, pulling the tabs out of my purse. I should put them back before he finds them missing. Coffee first. My head is killing too much to think about much more than coffee.

As I walk out of my room, my e-portal goes off. I know it's a wrong number without even checking. No one ever calls me. Leaving it buzzing on the floor, I head downstairs for my little cup of clarity.

Tobias

The sun hits me square in the face. My bloodshot eyes don't even flinch. They're too dried out to care.

I have been up all night replaying the image of them together over and over again. Each time I think about his hands covering her body, I get more and more volatile. I want to hit him, hard.

Instead, I slam my fist into a pillow. *How could he do that?* And then leave her there like some animal he hunted down?

"Tobias?" Mom calls from the other side of my door.

I open the door faster than she was clearly expecting. Her hand raises to her chest. I scared her.

"You're up?" she huffs.

"So are you."

She frowns at me. "That's because your friend just woke me up. He was pounding on the door to let him in. I'm surprised you didn't hear him."

"Hawk is here?"

"And before my morning tea." She shakes her head in mock frustration before she grows serious. "He said it couldn't wait until school started. You'd better see what he wants. He doesn't look too hot." She grabs my arm and practically shoves me down the stairs.

When I see Hawk, anger burns in my veins. I square my shoulders and scowl at him, waiting for his confession.

"She won't answer my calls, Tobs." His voice is firm, as though that one statement explains it all. It strikes me then that Hawk's never really been refused anything he's wanted before. Judging from his rigid posture, he doesn't care for that.

"Who won't call you?" I ask, even though I know who he means. I need to hear him say it. I need him to confirm that what I smelled last night really was him.

"Jada."

My nostrils flare involuntarily.

Although Mom hasn't made a peep since shoving me down the stairs, I know she's up there now listening from just around the hall. I have to contain myself, for the moment.

"Hawk, it's five o'clock in the morning," I say. "Maybe she's sleeping, like I was five minutes ago," I lie. "Or maybe she just missed the call. You're overreacting."

He snorts a deep guttural snort. "There's no way someone sleeps through or misses fifty-eight calls." His head shakes so slowly that it's eerie. "I know what she's doing. She's trying to ignore me. But it won't work." The tint of his bloodshot eyes makes him look almost evil.

I shove him into the living room, hoping Ma won't hear us in there.

"Fifty-eight times? Hawk, that's insanity. No wonder she's not taking your call."

His head whips around as he glares at me. "She's *mine,* Tobias." He shoves past me, hitting my shoulder and slamming me into the wall. "She just doesn't know it yet. But she will," he warns to no one in particular. Before I can even process what he just said, he storms out the room and into the morning.

Pissed, I follow after him. When we're both tucked safely into the woods, I can't hold it in any longer.

"Did you rape her?" I hiss.

Hawk stops mid-step and turns to look at me. His head cocks to the side.

"That *was* you I heard in the woods last night. You sick pervert!" He rushes toward me and throws a swing, which I just barely manage to dodge.

"Answer the question!" I shout.

His eyes bulge at the volume of my voice. He's afraid someone will hear us.

"No," he spits.

"Then why did you leave her alone in the woods like that?"

A growl escapes his lips.

"Did you touch her?" Hawk asks slowly, as though he's doing everything in his power to hold himself back.

"I made sure she got home safe, asshole." His fist doesn't miss its mark this time and I sink to my knees.

"That's for thinking I'd rape the woman I am going to marry," he spits as I gasp for breath. "Not that it's any of your business, but I left her there because she asked me to. She said she wanted to stay out and look at the stars." He takes a few steps away from me as I start to attempt to get up. "I thought you were my friend," he whispers. The bridge of his nose crinkles before he turns around and leaves me there broken on the ground, just as he had with Jada.

Jada

Things do not improve after coffee, because there is no coffee. Dad, of course, neglected to add it to his e-cart but somehow remembered vodka. So much for staying sober.

Let the fun begin.

With my head in my hands, I fumble around the house opening random drawers, searching for anything that might have caffeine in it. My search only produces a melt-away tab of aspirin and a handful of what I think are chocolate covered raisins. Cringing, I stick the tab against my tongue and chase it down with the mystery blobs. Even after chewing, I'm still not sure what they are, but at least part of it had chocolate.

"There," I mumble to the empty kitchen. "Headache and breakfast all in one."

Aside from Dad's snores, the house is mercifully quiet which will help the battle raging inside my head.

The safest time to be around Dad is when he's asleep. I tip-toe into his room to drop the pills back behind the dresser. The envelope makes the tiniest of crinkles as the bottle slides in and I hold my breath.

"Jeanne?"

I whip around to find my Dad sitting up in his bed. My heart stops.

"Jeanne, baby. Why did you leave me?" That's when I see his eyes are still safely closed. He's sleep-talking. He hasn't done that in years. I slink backwards against a wall, praying he doesn't discover me. I can't even think about what he'd do to me if he woke up now and found me in his room.

"It's all her fault, Jeanne. It's all her fault." Nausea consumes me. If he finds me now, I'm be a goner. I pull my limbs in close and hold my breath until his breathing becomes steady and the snoring begins again. With my belly to the ground, I crawl out of his room and into my own, closing the curtain behind me.

That was a close call.

I crawl into my bed and start to shake. *Why are things so messed up? Why can't I just have a normal life?* It isn't fair. Gah! Life sucks.

Beside me my cursed e-port goes off again, which I ignore. This time, however, a recording sounds.

"Incoming call limit met," it announces

cheerfully.

Incoming calls met? That's impossible. I can get up to sixty calls a day.

I kick around my clothes on the floor until I find the bag I had last night and dump everything right out onto my bed. The blood-red device stands out among the other captives from my bag: an apple core (gross), my scan card (though I never actually have any money in my account to buy anything), the balled up remains of a gum wrapper and a pair of socks (why I keep those in there I have no idea).

Touching the screen, the e-port comes to life and reports that I do, indeed, have sixty incoming calls. Scanning through the list of missed calls, I notice they are all from the same number.

"Who the hell is calling me?" I say to the phone. I touch the screen and listen to the messages.

"Jada, it's Hawk. I just wanted to say I had an amazing time with you last night."

Hawk...last night? I didn't see him last night.

My heart starts to pound as my fingers reach up to my lips. I swallow hard. Fractured bits of memories start to replay in my mind: my hands in someone's hair, teeth crashing together, arms pinning my hands over my head and me...*me*, begging him to touch me.

"Oh my God." I drop the e-port and bolt to the bathroom and bring up what little is in my stomach.

"That didn't really happen," I gag on the words. "Did it?"

Again, images bubble up: Hawk's hands cupping my breasts and my back arched up, inviting him in.

I dry heave again.

Like a zombie, I walk back into my room and pick up the phone. Sitting on my bed, I play the rest of the messages.

"Jada, I can't stop thinking of you. You taste like nothing I've ever had before and I want more. Need more. Please. Call me."

I'm shaken by the blatant hunger in his voice.

I skip forward a few messages as my brain tries to put the night back together.

"Why aren't you answering my calls? Pick up!"

Fear tingles down my spine as I skip ahead some more.

"I know you're there, Jada. I'm standing right outside your window; now pick up the damn phone!"

Gasping, I run to look out my window. I breathe a sigh of relief when I see he's not there.

I jump to the end of the messages, too stunned to think straight.

"Look, I'm sorry, all right. It's just that... you're the one, the girl I've been waiting for my whole life and now that I've found you, I can't bear to let you go. I love you, Jada. Do you hear me? I love you."

I stop playing the messages and delete all but that last one. He said he loves me.

Me.

It doesn't matter one iota that I don't love him. The only thing that matters is that he loves me. And as much as I hate to admit it, it feels nice.

I even have a soft smile on my face when I

carve this morning's letter into my flesh.

Tobias

I walk to school at the start of the year without Hawk for the first time since we were five. *Screw him.* Whatever he did to Jada last night has severed our friendship. There's no hope of repairing it now, not after what he did.

Even so, I leave the house about twenty minutes after I see Hawk leave. I don't want to chance him catching up to me.

Of course it takes me longer than most to get to school, so by the time I actually make it there, the campus is abuzz with students filtering into the school. There are kids shouting out their hellos to friends missed over the summer, cliques reforming and recruiting. It's not surprising that no one is shouting out my name. That is, until someone does.

"Tobias!"

Even without turning around, I know it's *her* running towards me. The hair lifting off my body is all the confirmation I need. I clench my hands tight around my bag, hoping that will make them stay put. My feet, however, start to turn toward her without me actually telling them to. When my head lifts up to find her, I don't bother to trying to look away. It's pointless to resist the pull she has on me.

The moment we lock eyes she stops running and stares at me. She pants a bit to catch her breath. Each exhalation carries her scent to me. It makes my knees go soft.

She's only ten feet away from me, but my body is begging to be closer, insisting on it. I actually have to lean backwards to stop from being pushed straight into her.

"What do you want?" I ask, hurt pouring out in the question laced with accusation.

Jada opens her mouth to speak but pauses there. Her brain seemingly trying to form the words she wants to say.

"Have you seen Hawk?" she finally spits out. His name is like an arrow to the gut.

Hawk. Of course, she's looking for him. Even after what he did, she's still wants him.

"No. I haven't seen him." I try to leave but her answer catches me off guard.

"Good," she says, letting out a great mouthful of air.

"Good?"

Her face contorts, giving the impression that she's conflicted about something.

Ignoring my question she says, "I think he might be mad at me." *Is that fear I see in her eyes?* My fists clench on their own accord.

"Why would he be mad at you?"

She turns away from me. My insides ache from her apparent rejection.

"He called me a few times and I didn't answer. I didn't know it was him," she whispers. "I thought it was a wrong number."

Like a fool, I ask, "Would you have taken the calls if you'd known it was him?"

She turns back to me, her deep brown eyes piercing into mine, searching for something. An eternity could have passed as we stare at each other and I wouldn't notice. When she finally closes her lids, I am winded. This girl literally takes my breath away.

"I don't know," she finally says.

"Well, you'd better figure it out soon." I say, stung beyond belief. I nod over her head. "Here he comes." Her eyes widen and when she turns to look for him, I use that as my chance to rip my feet away from her pull. There is no way I'm about to stick around now that Hawk is here.

I march into the school without so much as a backward glance. *Good riddance to both of them.*

Jada

I can feel Tobias walking away from me and his withdrawal feels so raw that I almost gasp. Gazing into his eyes, I could tell that he had wanted me to say 'no' when he asked about Hawk's calls. Did that mean that Tobias was jealous? Is that what I saw in his eyes just now? Is he jealous of Hawk? Could Tobias actually like me?

No Jada. Stop it. Do not fall for Tobias! Falling for Tobias would be as easy as breathing and as painful as death when it eventually ended. Because it would. That much I know for certain. Sooner or later, love stops. People cheat, fall out of love or die. But in the end, the result is the same. Love is finite. I'm not about to set myself up for that sort of heartbreak.

As Hawk approaches me, my heart starts to thrum. It's a vastly different sensation than when I'm near Tobias, though. This is a thrum of...warning?

"Jada, we need to talk. Now." Hawk says, taking me by the arm and pulling me off the to edge of the school property. No one either sees or cares that I'm being dragged away by him.

It is only once we're in the woods that he goes off on me.

"Why didn't you pick up last night?" There is a dangerous fire in his ice blue eyes. I realize there is only one way to put out that heat, so I do my best to imagine those cold eyes getting darker, warmer, like the color of mahogany. If I squint, Hawk's hard jaw softens around the edges. I pretend his blonde waves become a sea of chocolate curls. Standing on tip-toes, I lean in and kiss Hawk but taste only Tobias.

Instantly, I feel his anger melt away. He pulls me in closer to him, practically crushing me, but I don't flinch. The pain reminds just me to stay numb, to keep pretending.

Eventually, he yanks his lips from mine. There is still a touch of fury etched along his forehead.

Holding my chin firmly in his hand he asks me again, slower this time. "Why didn't you answer my calls?"

Instinctively, I know I have to answer this question very carefully. I have to answer it the way he wants it to be answered.

"I didn't know it was you. I thought you were a prank caller. If I had known it was you..." I say, with my very breakable jaw still tight in his grasp.

"If you'd known it was me, what?" He releases the pressure on my chin but only by a fraction. A small grin touches the corner of his mouth. "I want to hear you say it."

Heat burns in my eyes at his blatant order, but I don't see a safe alternative. We are completely out of eyesight of anyone who can help if this ends badly, and I am very aware of the pressure he's still exerting on my chin. "If I had known it was you, I would have taken your calls. All sixty of them." The lie almost catches in my throat.

His half-grin grows more complete and he releases my face. It's all I can do not to rub the pain away. I won't give him the satisfaction of knowing he's hurt me.

"So now that you have my number you're out of excuses not to answer the next time I call." His hands slide down my back and over my butt where they land and anchor themselves. "Right?" he whispers hot against my ear.

"Right."

He kisses me again, but this time it's different. Even though his lips feel the same crushed against mine, I know intuitively what this kiss is: he has officially marked his territory.

What did I just do?

Chapter 9

Tobias

I plow my way past kids crowding the hallways and manage to find my science class even though my thoughts are focused on something else entirely. I don't want to admit it, but I'm worried. I left her alone with Hawk practically charging at her, and I did nothing to protect her from his overt anger.

She's not my problem though. She's chosen Hawk, so let her find out for herself the jerk he's turned into.

Not. My. Problem.

Too bad my gut doesn't agree with me. I've been on edge ever since I left her.

Needing something to keep my mind occupied, I grab an e-board from the front of the room and log in for class: *Modern Myths and How Science Quells the Mystery Behind Them.*

I click open the syllabus for the year trying to get a sense of how much work it'll be. Science is one of my better subjects, so I'm guessing the class will be a cake walk.

The year is broken down into trimesters: Ancient Buildings using Modern Technology, Beyond the Final Frontier and Unexplained Oddities. The first two trimesters look like more of the same-old-same-old: the explanation of pyramids and other structures humans can't fathom the poor primitive man could have built by hand, followed by the recent discovery of other 'Earth like' planets and how that's shaking up the science field. But the Unexplained Oddities section is strange. Dragging my hand across the board, I pull up the reading list for it:

Better off Dead? Ghosts and the Beyond
Soul Mates in Flames: How Science Fails to Explain These Bizarre Human Connections
Vampires and Werewolves: The Truth Behind the Fangs
* Why There is No Fountain of Youth.*

One of the titles sets off an army of bells: *Soul Mates in Flames.* I click on the link and the file begins to download. Other students are starting to trickle in, but I ignore them. Hyperlinked throughout the file are hundreds of links to other sites on the topic, but I don't open any of them. I'm searching for something. I just don't know what.

My eyes scan the document stopping briefly on the word Soul Mates. When I touch the word, the definition pops up:

"A person or persons with whom your soul has met in another life: uncles, sisters, parents, occasionally lovers but this term should not be confused with it's rarer expression of Twin Flames."

Twin Flames...where have I heard that term before?

I click on the link only to get an error code.

'Error-File requested has not been uploaded at this time. Please check back later.'

Cursing under my breath, I turn the board off in frustration. When I look up, the room has filled and the front screen is on, projecting our instructor, Mr. Harper.

"Morning, class," the man on the screen says. "Welcome to Modern Myths. If you thought this would be easier than taking Quantitative Decision Making, you were wrong." The corners of Mr. Harper's lips curl into a grin. "Those with weak study habits had best leave now."

Behind me, two students gather their things before scooting out the door, moving off to the side just as another student enters.

My gut twists. It's Jada.

Instantly my body is reacting to her presence as hers seems to be to mine. She stands in the doorway, not moving, as though she's stuck in mud.

"Please take out your tablets, log in and review the syllabus." Mr. Harper's voice booms across the room, shaking me back into my senses. "Any questions before we dive in?" I feel my hand shoot up into the air.

"Ah, yes, Tobias, isn't it? What's your question?"

My eyes stay glued to Jada. She has

managed to slide into a chair closest to the door, as though that was as far as she could get her body to move. Her eyes don't budge from mine. "What are Twin Flames?" I hear myself ask.

"Ah, you've been reading ahead," Mr. Harper says. "Well, since you asked, Twin Flames are said to be created when a soul is ripped apart by some tragic event, creating two halves of the *same* soul: one part male, the other female. Those half-souls, if you will, in theory, are believed to spend eternities searching for their missing half. Their souls are never complete until they are bonded together once more."

"That sounds *so* romantic," I hear a girl up front giggle.

"Romantic, perhaps, but often times tragic," Mr. Harper cautions. Both Jada and I turn to look at him.

"Tragic, why?" the girl asks.

Mr. Harper shrugs. "There isn't a lot of scientific data on Twin Flames, but what we do have, amazingly almost always ends in some sort of dreadful demise of the reunited souls. It's almost as though there is another force tasked at keeping the souls apart." Mr. Harper pauses, seemingly lost in thought. "In fact, there is some debate as to whether or not a pair of Twin Flames happened right here in Webster a few years back. But I'll save that tidbit for our third trimester. For now we need to focus on our first unit: Ancient Buildings Using Modern Technology."

He continues on with his lecture, but I don't hear a single word. I can't hear or see a single thing except her, my Twin Flame.

Jada

No, I hiss at myself. *You will not fall for this stupidity. There is no such thing as Twin Flames! Now, stop looking at Tobias.*

But, of course, my eyes refuse to move off his. How easy it would be to fool myself into thinking that someone had been made just for me. I'll have to be extremely careful. One kiss, just one kiss from Tobias, and I could easily lose myself inside the promise of what he might bring.

A rapid string of beeps comes across the screen just then, bringing me back to reality. Principal Notices like this one are common in all schools. Most of them are trivial things, like reminding people to return school e-portals or telling us about a blocked site, but this one is a first for me. It's a weather warning.

"Good morning, everyone," a stern Mrs. Wellington says from the screen. Mr. Harper's image shrinks down onto a smaller screen at the bottom. He looks a bit annoyed that the announcement is taking up his class time.

"As you are all aware, the news has been reporting a potentially dangerous storm headed our way. Well, now it appears that it's moving faster than predicted. They think it will hit us tomorrow morning, but perhaps sooner." She clears her throat; public speaking is clearly not her strong suit. "They are urging everyone to take proper shelter as the air quality could become dangerously low. Accordingly, we are closing today at noon in order to get you all home safely before the storm hits. Please check your notifications to see if school will be held tomorrow or not."

Just like that, her image is gone and Mr. Harper's comes back to the full screen.

There is an excited buzz flying around the room, but all I feel is panic. If they're letting us out of school because of the air quality, it means Tobias' health is in danger.

Although no one else would be able to tell, I notice Tobias' jaw harden. He's worried and now so am I.

As soon as the clock hits ten o'clock, the overhead bell dings, and Mr. Harper releases us to our next class. Everyone but Tobias and me, head out the door. His eyes are boring holes into his desk. His body has become rigid, almost as though he doesn't trust himself to move.

I know the feeling. My limbs seem to be disobeying me at the moment as well. I should be walking out the door like everyone else instead of walking right up to him. My feet just won't listen to me. They stop right in front of his desk, practically pinning me there.

"Hey," I mumble. *Hey? That's the best you've got?* "So I was just making sure you were all set with the storm and all."

"I'll be just ducky," comes his clipped reply.

His hostility towards me is completely unnecessary. "What's your problem? I was just trying to be nice!"

"Yeah, well I don't think Hawk would approve of you talking to me, so you'd better run along."

"Hawk? What does he have to do with this?" He is making no sense.

Tobias glares at me. "Everything," he says,

pushing out of his chair.

"I don't understand."

He gets about a step away from me before he stops. "Let's just say he wasn't happy that I brought you home last night."

My mouth goes dry.

"Wait. *You* took me home?" My head is desperately trying to remember, but it's coming up blank.

For a moment, he's the one who looks confused. Other students start filtering into the class. "We can't talk here." He looks over his shoulder. "Follow me."

He storms out of the room, and I have to struggle to keep up with him. His head bobs in and out of a sea of students pushing to get to their next class, but I stay with him until he disappears into an unused classroom.

Following after him, I give a quick look behind me just to make sure we weren't seen. As soon as I'm inside, he closes the door. Standing face to face with him, I can feel the heat rolling off his body. My mouth waters looking at the soft curve of his lips. Pinching his eyes closed, he backs away from me a bit, and I have to work hard not to follow after him. The urge to be closer to him is potent in a close space like this.

"What sort of game are you playing?" he snaps at me.

I blink. "Game?"

"Last night... " he begins, but then stops himself.

"Were you there?" My voice is terribly small. I sink down into one of the chairs, not sure if I'm prepared to hear what he's going to say.

"Was I there? Are you serious?" He sounds angry at me.

Suddenly, I'm embarrassed. I'm going to have to tell him the truth.

"Look, this isn't something I'm proud of but I slipped a few of my dad's pills last night for my nerves. All I remember is going into the woods to cool off and then waking up with a really bad headache."

His mouth opens and then closes. "Are you telling me you don't remember what you did last night?"

I start shaking my head. "What *did* I do?" The panic is evident in my voice.

Tobias looks like he's about to fall apart. "I don't know." He swallows. "But I found you alone. In the woods." He clears his throat. "Naked."

I start pacing. My fears are being confirmed, and I'm having a really hard time processing it. "No. No. That was just a dream. That didn't really happen." *If I say it enough it will be true.*

Tobias takes the smallest of steps closer to me. "Jada, what do you think you dreamed?"

The intensity in his eyes makes it impossible for me to lie.

"That I was kissing you."

For a second his eyes brighten and then they cloud over just as fast.

"Well it wasn't a dream," he says, walking towards the door. "And it sure as hell wasn't me."

I feel like I've been punched in the gut. The look on his face--he thinks I'm a whore. Hell, maybe I am. Doing my best to holding back the tears that are burning just beneath the surface, I try to push past him, but his hand juts out, stopping me.

"I'm sorry. That was a dick-headed thing to say."

"Yeah, it was." I fumble with the edge of my shirt, wishing I could dissolve into its darkness. "Did I..." I swallow hard. "Did I sleep with him?"

"I don't know."

I hang my head even lower.

"But I don't think so. At least from the story he gave me."

"What did he tell you?"

His face shifts. "I asked him if he...took...advantage of you. He said no and then proceeded to punch me in the gut."

"What?" I gasp.

He takes a tiny step closer to me, and it makes me shiver.

"Be careful, Jada. He's changed. It's like a switch has gone off since he met you. He's not the Hawk I grew up with. He seems..."

"Dangerous," I finish.

Tobias stiffens. "Did he do something to you?"

The protectiveness of his question is jarring so I try to soothe him. "I'm a big girl. I can take care of myself."

"Like you did last night?" he snaps.

My mouth drops open, but no words escape my lips. That's the second cruel thing he's said to me.

I push past him and out the door, ignoring both the pull of him and his shouts of apology.

Screw him.

I don't need this, any of this. Rounding the corner of the hall, I decide to just cut my losses and go home.

That was my plan until I plow right into a rock hard body.

"Whoa, shouldn't you be in class?" Hawk grins, pulling me into his arms. The way he's looking at me renders me speechless, but I do manage to take a few steps away from him until he backs me straight into the wall. Hawk looks at me, waiting for an answer to the question he asked me.

"I got lost," I whisper.

"Good thing I found you then." His smirk turns dangerous as he lowers his lips to mine, blocking out my protest. His weight pins me to the wall. I'm helpless to push him off and he knows it, leaning into me harder.

"I missed you." Hawk smiles down at me, tracing the edge of my jaw with his thumb. I can't help but remember earlier when he held my face prisoner with those same hands that now show such tenderness. Maybe I mistook his rage for passion.

A greasy haired kid bumps into my shoulder pushing me further into his arms and something clicks inside me. Hawk will take care of me and love me. I don't have to be alone anymore. Better still, I can look him dead in the eyes without my insides melting, like they do with Tobias.

I snuggle into his chest as his lips touch my head.

Hawk is perfect for me.

Chapter 10

Tobias

After being a dick to Jada, I duck into the bathroom to splash cold water over my face. How could I be so mean to her? I all but called her a slut and, for all I know, Hawk could have taken advantage of her.

Gah, I'm such a prick!

I'm so ashamed of my behavior that I can't even risk her seeing me when the final bell rings, so I hide in the bathrooms until a janitor finally kicks me out so he can lock up.

I drag my feet down the steps of the school, beyond ashamed of what I've done to her. I was so cold to her. The last look she gave me is burned into my brain. I let her down and I hate myself for it.

The road is deserted as I walk home and I'm thankful for the quiet. I deserve to be alone right now, maybe forever. Peripherally, I check in on the sky. The clouds have started to form, but they are still far enough away that I can make it back home and plug into my nebulizer well before the rain even thinks of starting. To be safe though, I reach into my bag to grab my inhaler, but it's not there.

Hmm.

I pat my jeans, expecting to feel it there, but it's not. *Where the hell is it?* Stopping, I dump everything out of my bag. No inhaler. I must have left it inside the school, which is probably locked up by now. Cursing under my breath, I check the sky again. The clouds have taken on an odd yellowish-green tint.

A wave of dread runs down my spine. This storm is coming faster than I thought. What if I *don't* get home in time?

My heart starts to thunder along with the sky above. My breath becomes labored from panic. Trying to calm down, I exhale deeply. I just need to focus. *Just get your ass home before it rains, Tobias. That's all you need to do*, I chant.

I start to walk along the dirt road willing myself to both go faster and yet not push myself. I can't risk having an attack without an inhaler on me. Not with what's coming.

When I reach the halfway mark, I slow my pace a bit. So far the rain has held off. The air has gotten markedly thinner, making it harder to breathe, but it's the rain that's gonna be the bitch. Because of that nuclear plant meltdown, the oxygen count is expected to drop well below my lung capacity. I had a hard time believing the reports up until this very second. Already I feel like I'm breathing through oatmeal.

Guilt washes over me. Ma is probably worried sick about me right about now. I should have been home an hour ago. My e-port is dead so I can't even send word that I'm okay. I'm actually sort of surprised that Hawk hasn't come looking for me. I guess our friendship really is over.

Frustrated, I stop and rest. Placing my hands on my knees, I do my best to take deep breaths.

In. Out. In. Out. *Almost home, Tobias.*

That's when I hear it. If I didn't know better, I would swear it was a crowd going wild at one of Hawk's football games, but my gut knows exactly what it is. Slowly, I look over my shoulder and see it for myself. A giant wall of rain has begun about a mile down the road, and it's headed straight for me.

Run!

My feet propel themselves forward. With only seconds to spare, I duck into the woods, praying I can find shelter with a pocket of breathable air before it's too late.

Jada

The house moans as the wind from the storm slams against the siding. Not to be outdone, the rain throttles the tin roof, causing the power to flick on and off. A few more gusts like this and it will be out for the night.

Since Dad's passed out on the couch, a half a bottle of vodka gone, I do what I can to keep out the rain: lock the windows and doors and pray the roof holds.

As I'm dead-bolting the front door, I drop to my knees in pain.

The hairs on my arms rise...my gut twists.

Tobias.

My stomach churns again making me gasp. He's hurt.

Hurry, the wind seems to howl.

Without a jacket or even shoes I fly out the door and down the porch steps. The screen door bounces wildly against the house with the wind. I only hope it doesn't wake up Dad.

I'm drenched in a flash. Cold rain pelts against my skin so hard it feels like tiny shards of glass cutting into me. Numb to the pain, I run down the driveway and out onto the road. I look around frantically for signs of Tobias. It's raining so hard I can't see more than a few feet in front of me. When the lightning flashes I'm able to see for a fraction of a second. My feet feel like ice. I'm standing in a pool of water that has already begun to flood the road. A sense of dread slams into my chest. I'm never going to find him in this.

Desperate, I do the only thing I can think of: I yell out his name, over and over, each time more frantic than the last. I scream until my voice cracks. The woods around me absorb my cries.

The woods.

He's there. I know it.

"Tobias!" I screech. "I'm coming! Hold on!" I run as fast as I can across the mud-filled road and crash through the overgrowth lining the woods. I ignore the pain from the scratches the low branches carve into my skin.

The deafening sound of rain lessens a bit under the protection of the branches above. Somehow the ground here has yet to become soaked to the core. Instinctively, I seek out my rock. My feet find their way to it without the help of my brain. Trusting the pull, I allow myself to be dragged across the root-laden ground.

Lightning flashes again.

A dark figure is leaning against my rock.

"Tobias," I whisper.

He looks up at me, both relieved and scared. He's clutching at his sides. He's dying.

Within seconds, I am at his side.

"Where's your inhaler?" I scream, sinking down beside him. He's too weak to answer. He just closes his eyes in defeat.

No. You are not going to die on me.

"What should I do?" I wail at him.

He lifts his hand and slowly forms a curve. His fingers then form something that looks like a person walking. *What the hell is he doing?* Then he makes a fist. No, not a fist. His thumb is in front of his fingers...an R! He is signing the letter R. That curvy thing was a C, then a walking dude, then an R. C something R. *Shit!*

"CPR?" I gasp. "You need me to give you CPR?"

His eyes close in relief.

My heart swells. I could save him.

If only I knew CPR.

Tobias

One look at her soaked and ashen face and I realize she doesn't know how to do CPR. I give her a small smile trying to convey that I understand, that it isn't her fault. I try not to think about dying, but each breath is bringing less and less oxygen and I can feel myself slipping away.

Before I close my eyes against the crushing pressure in my lungs, I look up at her one last time. She is trembling and dripping wet. Knowing I can't do anything to comfort her is almost as painful as the lack of breath. I want to reach out and tell her that it will be okay, but I can't lie to her. Besides, I'm too weak to talk right now. I just want to sleep. Just close my eyes for one second...

That's when I feel her lips on mine, hot and electric. A literal jolt of life surges into me.

My eyes open. Her face is pressed against mine. Her drenched golden hair falls against my chest. But it's her breath that consumes me. It's warm and healing, filling my lungs with life. Her lips, pressed soft against mine, replenish my soul. An angel has come to save me, again.

Jada

It is working! His chest is rising and falling! Maybe I do know CPR after all! Maybe watching all those ER shows as a kid has paid off. Cocky, I move my hands over his chest ready to start compressions, but his hand touches mine. Heat surges all over my body. I look down at him, crumpled on the ground and he shakes his head, then points back to his mouth.

For a second I think he wants me to kiss him, then I realize what he's trying to say. He doesn't need chest compressions. His heart is still beating. He just needs air, you moron!

Feeling foolish, I bend back over him, pinch his nose shut and give him another series of breaths. As I press my mouth to his, I try to ignore how soft his lips really are. Hawk was right. They *are* soft: like silk, burning hot silk, and familiar. Achingly familiar.

Without actually meaning to, my breathing somehow turns into kissing. It starts as a soft peck at first but after that taste I want more. Need more.

Hungry now, I move my lips to his again, more urgently than the last time. His lips respond to me, melding with mine perfectly. My hands dig into his hair, lifting him off the ground so I can straddle him. His hands press into my hips, locking me on top of his body. When his tongue brushes against mine, I almost lose my mind.

When a small cough escapes Tobias' lips, however, my trance is broken. I rip my lips away and force myself off him. Still coughing, Tobias pulls himself up to lean back against the rock. His breath is labored, but he seems okay.

We sit together in silence for a moment, listening to the rain pelt against the trees. I keep a close eye on his chest, making sure it's still moving. The trees have done a decent job blocking of the rain, but he won't last much longer out here. He needs to get to a doctor, fast.

"That's twice you've saved my life now," Tobias says, coughing a bit.

"Let's not try for three, okay?"

His hand reaches out and cradles my face. My eyes rise up meet his.

"Thank you," he whispers again. His voice is low, husky and sexy as hell.

His hand is cold and shriveled from the rain, but his touch is like fire. It's both comforting and confusing. The ache in my chest returns and pulls me forward. Foolishly, I lean in to kiss him again. One kiss, I tell myself, I just need a tiny little taste of him.

He refuses to let my lips go when I try to pull away. His hands lace into the back of my hair, pulling me closer. A shiver of excitement runs down my spine.

When his tongue slides inside my mouth this time, I actually groan with delight. Somewhere in the back of my mind, I know I should stop. I'm probably making it harder for him to breathe, but by the way his hands slide around to cup my breasts, I can only assume he's getting along just fine.

He has me completely in his trance, this boy I hardly know.

It's only when he starts coughing again that I realize he's not out of danger.

"Damn it," he coughs. "I'm sorry."

I run my hand down his chest and feel his heart beating wildly against my touch.

"It's not your fault. It's this storm. We've got to get you out of here."

"I know." He looks pissed at himself, probably angry that he can't even kiss without getting sick.

Undeterred, I stand up and reach down for his hand. "Lean on me. I'll get you out of here."

He clenches his teeth in understanding, and I feel his weight against me as I wrap my arm around his waist. Tobias rests his head on my shoulder, and I have to fight against the urge to do the same. His wheezing has returned a bit, and it's causing me to panic.

We take our time getting out of the woods even though he seems stronger. I don't want to risk a setback.

Once we're at the edge of the woods I look up at the sky. It's still raining.

"What do we do?" I ask Tobias, who is shaking against the cold.

He lets go of me for a second and starts to take off his shirt.

"What are you doing? It's freezing out here!"

He wrings out the water as best he can.

"I'll cover my mouth with this. It might help."

Nodding, I bring my arm back around his waist.

"On three?" I say. He gives me a weak nod.

"One. Two." *Please* don't let him die.

"Three."

Together we half-run, half-walk, straight past my house to Kari's.

Neither house has power, but Kari has a car, and right now that's all I care about.

"Ms. Philips! Kari! Please, I need help!" I yell, knocking her front door open with my foot. It is rude, but I don't have time for manners.

Her house is pitch black from the power outage. My teeth chatter against the fading warmth of the house.

Setting Tobias down on her couch, I pull one of those throws she has on all of her chairs to me and wrap it around him. I'm yanking a second from the couch when Kari comes around the corner with a candle in her hand.

"Good Lord in heaven! What's going on?"

"Kari, we need to borrow your car. He needs to go the hospital!"

Kari looks at Tobias who is shaking and dripping all over her couch.

"What's wrong with him?"

I start to tear up. "It's his asthma. He doesn't have his inhaler and this stupid rain has made it harder for him to breathe."

Kari walks closer to Tobias bringing the light of the flame with her. The blue tint of his skin is returning, causing a wave of nausea to flood over me.

"Your mama's a nurse, right?" Kari asks Tobias. He nods weakly.

Kari puts her hands on her hips. "Then I'm taking you home. I know where he lives," she tells me, grabbing her coat.

"Home? No wait, he needs to go to the hospital!" I shriek.

She turns on me, her eyes dark. "I am *not* stepping foot into another hospital." Her voice shakes when she says this, which makes me step away in shock.

"Tobias, do you have stuff at home that can help this?" She gestures to his chest.

He nods again. Kari turns to me.

"Think about it, darling. If I take him to a hospital, he's gonna have to wait, maybe hours before he gets the medicine he needs. Let's get him home, get him some meds right away. If his she needs him to see a doc after that, I'll drive them there. Got it?"

I bite my lip, hating that she's right. On a night like tonight, the ERs will be filled with people needing help or at least thinking they do. Emergencies always bring out the crazies.

"Okay, fine," I say, resolved. "Let's go." I start

to help Tobias up, but her hand comes down on my shoulder.

"You're not coming, Jada." Kari says, firmly. "You need to go home, before your father finds out you're not there." Her eyes pierce into me. "I don't want you to get in trouble for sneaking out." I wonder suddenly if she's overheard our arguments before.

I stomp my feet on the ground in frustration. I hate that Kari is right. If I'm not at home when Dad gets up, after everything he's had to drink, there will be marks on me that I won't be able to hide in the morning.

Tobias brushes my hand with his and my fears melt. "I'll be fine, Jada," he says, standing up on his own. "Honest. I just need my nebulizer. Besides, my mom's not going to be happy with me leaving the house. Probably better if you didn't see that." He gives me a small smile.

Kari jerks her head to the door in a not so subtle hint to hit the road.

"He's gonna be fine, honey. You go home now."

I give one last look to Tobias who gives me a weak smile before I turn and look at Kari. She's turned herself around to   look at her wall of photos.

"Please, please don't let this happen again," she whispers to the wall.

I take that as my cue to leave.

Tobias

Kari stares dead ahead along the road

towards my house. I don't ask how she knows where I live. It's a small town. Everybody knows everybody.

"I'm sorry," I wheeze. "I didn't mean to cause her..." Wheeze. "...trouble."

Her lips form a hard line. "That girl was in trouble the minute she laid eyes on you." She turns to glare at me.

"Trouble?" I cough out.

Her shoulders slump and she lets out a big sigh. She shifts gears and pulls onto the dirt road that leads to my house. Her hands stay firmly planted on the wheel as though she's trying to control herself.

Kari narrows her eyes at me. "Have you ever seen two people in your life that you knew deep down in your gut that they were meant to be together?" she asks. I start to answer, but she holds up her hand to stop me. "Now, I'm not just talking about a puppy dog crush. I'm talking about the kind of love that consumes your entire body, takes you hostage. A feeling so powerful that it makes you do or say anything, just to be near them? Almost like you're being physically pulled towards them?" She glances over at me to get my reaction.

My mouth opens to say no, but it's a lie. That's *exactly* how it is with Jada.

"That's what I thought," she says grimly. "Jada does that to you, doesn't she?"

I start coughing, surprised at her perceptiveness. "I never said that."

Kari shakes her head. "You didn't have to. It's plain as day when you two look at each other." She pulls into my driveway and cuts the engine before looking me dead in the eyes. "And that is *exactly* the reason you need to stay away from her."

"What?"

"Now, I know this doesn't make any sense. You're too young and stupid to think that anything bad could come from loving someone so much that it hurts." A candle flickers upstairs and then vanishes. Ma must have seen us pull in. I know I should go in, but I can tell Kari has more she needs to say.

"In college," she finally says, "I had a friend who fell that hard for a boy. His name was Etash." Her voice starts to waver. "The day the two of them met, it was like lighting came down from the heavens. I have never seen two people more in love than those two were. For one brief moment they were happy." A small smile creeps onto her face for a second before it vanishes. "Since then I've learned that sort of happiness comes at a cost."

"Thanks for the warning," I say reaching for the door handle.

But before I can get out of the car, her hand is on my arm. "Your friend, Hawk. He has blue eyes, right?"

"Um, yeah. Why?"

She closes her eyes, like I've punched her. "Like the color of ice." It's not a question.

"I guess you could say that. So what?"

She nods her head slowly. "It'll be him. He will take her away from you." Her eyes are wide now.

I start to cough. I need my meds, but her gaze is so intense that it's frozen me to the seat.

"Don't trust him," she pleads.

"Tobias!" The door beside me rips open. Ma is standing out in the rain. Her face is covered in fear.

"He needs help, Ms. Garret. I found him out on the road. I knew you could help him faster than that damn hospital. You call me, though, if you need a lift there."

Ma nods her thanks, grabs my arm and starts to pull me out of Kari's car. My lungs cough against the night, but I can't help and glance back at Kari one last time. She's hunched over the wheel, crying.

Chapter 11

Jada

As soon as Kari's car pulls out of the drive with Tobias, I spring from our kitchen window where I have kept vigil since she kicked me out of her house. Dad's still passed out on the couch. I've got another hour easily, judging by that snore. The only good part about her kicking me back home is at least I've been able to get some dry clothes on. It would be just like me to die of pneumonia after tonight's ordeal.

Checking on Dad once more, I sneak back out of the house and run over to Kari's. I need to be there when she returns. I need to make sure Tobias is okay. If he is all right, then I can take whatever punishment Dad can dish out.

Although the rain has stopped, the wind has kicked up, making me wrap my arms around my body for warmth. A gust cuts right through me, blowing Kari's front door wide open. She must not have shut it all the way when they left.

Instead of just shutting the door, I opt to go in. After all, it's freezing out here.

Closing the door quietly behind me, I stand in the hall.

"Kari?" I ask her dark house.

There is no answer. *Of course there isn't an answer you moron, you just saw her drive off!*

A light flicks on in her kitchen, causing me to jump. *Chill out Jada the power must have just kicked back on.* Still spooked, I tiptoe into her living room as though the walls might tattle on me if I make too much noise.

Even now, that damn picture calls to me. In the dim light from the kitchen, I can tell his dark eyes watch me, begging me to remember something. Eventually I turn away, ashamed that I can't see what he wanted me to see.

I venture into the safety of the kitchen where I can escape the picture's pull. It's only when I see Kari's table that I realize that he is still calling to me. Covering the kitchen table are piles and piles of photos albums. Amid all the pages laid open, *his* eyes find me. The hairs on my neck stand up. My feet pull me to the table. A yellowed newspaper clipping with his face looks back at me.

My eyes dance down to read the article.

Webster Journal
The Circle of Life--Times Three
Tragedy mixes with miracles at Webster General Hospital

October 14, 2011

Tragedy struck late Sunday night at the Webster General Hospital in Webster, NH, when three teens were killed in what appears to be a twisted love triangle. Naya Adams, 18, of New York, Etash Kapur, 19, of New Jersey and Seth Falconer, 18, of Webster, were all pronounced dead Sunday evening.

According to Detective Simons of the Webster Police Department, Falconer, Adams' ex-boyfriend, allegedly kidnapped and drugged Adams, causing her to overdose. When Adams' new boyfriend, Kapur, arrived on the scene, Falconer punctured Kapur's left lung with a butcher knife before killing himself with his father's shotgun. Doctors tell us that Kapur rallied until the ambulance arrived shortly thereafter, but ultimately suffocated to death on his own blood. Simons said the murders happened in the home of Falconer's parents, Douglas and Natalie Falconer, who were out of town when the events occurred. At press time, they had no comment.

Distraught family and friends arrived at the ER in shock about the night's events. One teen, Kari Philips, 18, had this to say about the death of her college friend. "I had no idea how cruel Seth was. I knew she was scared of him, but no one knew what he was capable of."

In a twist of fate, that same night in the NICU unit just above the ER, three babies were born: Jada Williams, Tobias Garrett and Hawk Sanders. Nurses on the scene called their births on such a tragic night, "a miracle."

Not everyone present, however, saw the events the same way. The grandmother of Kapur had this to say: "My grandson may have died tonight, but not his soul. It has moved on." She went on to say, "It was no accident that three *babies were born on the same night those three teens died. It was fate."*

The parents of the 'miracle babies' were unavailable for comment.

I have to read the article several times before the depth of what I'm reading sinks in. The reminder that he died makes tears form in my eyes. But even more confusing is that Kari was there the day he died...the day I was born...

"I thought I told you to go home." Kari's voice startles me.

"Oh!" I snap my head up, knocking over a cold cup of tea that had been perched on the table. It shatters into oblivion at my feet.

"I'm sorry. I'll clean that up," I say.

"Leave it."

Standing, I look down at the article then back at her. "You were there. You were at the hospital when..."

Kari crosses her arms with a scowl etched onto her face. "When my best friend died? Yeah. I was there. And your being born on that day was no damn miracle. It was a curse."

My skin grows cold at the seriousness in her voice. "What do you mean?"

She sighs but then pulls out a chair. "I think it's time you and I had a talk."

Tobias

As soon as I'm inside, Mom kicks me up the stairs to put on my nebulizer. The second it's turned on she surrounds me with my ratty old blanket, which she does every time I get sick, and cocoons me in its warmth. Tonight, I don't object.

"Not a peep out of you for an hour." Mom says, pulling up the rocker, guarding me.

"I'm okay, Mom!" I say through the mask trying to soothe her, but she's not having it.

"Wanna make it two?" She raises her eyebrows up to the ceiling.

Shaking my head, I hunker down and let my medicine do its thing. As soon as the hour is up, however, I pull the mask down.

Mom's face is pinched tight. She's been rocking away, fretting this whole time, and now it looks like she's about to explode.

"That's it!" she yells, getting up from the rocker. "You're not leaving this house again!"

"Mom, I'm fine." I try to sit up but she pushes my shoulder down.

She starts to pace the floor. The wood is worn where she steps. It's a path she's walked a million times worrying about me.

"This is not a discussion right now. I'm going to get someone to cover my shifts the rest of this week. After that...I don't know what's gonna happen. But you are not to step foot out of this house until you get cleared by a doctor. You hear me? Not one little toe!"

Her eyes have started to well up with tears, so I know she's worried about me. I can't even count the number of times she's almost lost me, but she can't keep me inside, not now. Not after I've found Jada.

"Ma, you know what the doctors are gonna say. They can't help me anymore. They've done everything they can. You just have to let me be happy with what time I have left."

"Don't you talk like them." Her voice trembles. "You're getting stronger everyday. You'll show them."

"If you keep me tied to this machine for the rest of my days, I won't want to live anymore."

It hurt to say it, but she needs to know she can't keep me safe forever.

She sinks back into the chair. Tears fall from her eyes.

"When you didn't come home after school with Hawk, and those dark clouds rolled in..." She starts to fan herself with her hands. "I kept watching the news, and they kept saying how bad the air quality was getting. How it came faster than they predicted..." Ma starts pacing the floor in her white nurses' shoes, evidently too stressed about me to change once she got home.

"I didn't mean to worry you." I hang my head, ashamed.

Mom sits down beside me and pats my pale arm with her dark hand. "Boy, you've been giving me gray hairs ever since the day I first held you."

Her face softens a bit at the memory. From past stories, I know she was working as a nurse the night I was born and then later adopted me when my real parents couldn't afford my medical care.

"Mom, do you think Jada and Hawk are meant to be together?" I'm not sure why I ask her that. It just slips out.

Instead of seeing the pity that I expect to see in her eyes, I see anger.

"No," she says. "No, I do not."

That surprises me.

"Um, why not? I mean, it is strange how they found each other again after all this time... "

Mom stands up again and walks to my door.

"Don't budge. I need to show you something." She hovers in the doorway, as though she's not sure if she can walk through it.

Completely confused, I watch her leave my room and hear her go downstairs. I push myself up to sit upright and take another few inhalations of my mist.

When Mom finally returns, she's got something tucked in her arms. She hugs the maroon book close to her chest. Its edges are lined with dust and the pages have turned yellow. Sitting beside me, she opens the cover and strokes the back of her thumb along the photo that is set in inside cover.

"I'm not supposed to have this photo," she says quietly, as though someone would hear her and rip it out of her hands. "You weren't mine at the time you see, so I shouldn't have been taking pictures of you, but I couldn't help myself." She removes a yellowed envelope tucked deep inside of the album. She takes out a small picture that has been carefully placed there. She hands me the photo like it's made out of glass.

In the picture are two babies, side by side. They are curled right up to each other practically hugging the clear plastic that separates them.

"The two of you together was like nothing I'd ever seen before and I don't know, I guess I wanted to remember how pure and innocent it was."

"That's me?"

Mom nods. "And that's Jada."

My mouth opens as I look at the pink balled up baby next to my blue bundle.

"That's Jada?" I whisper, unable to believe it. I *had* met her before, but I was just too young to remember it.

"She lost her mama during childbirth. It was so sad. Those few days in the nursery you two bonded together like super glue. Lord, would you wail if I took her away from you." She laughs at the memory. "And she'd do the same if I took you from her." Mom sighs and takes the picture back. She traces her finger over our faces once before gently putting it back.

When she closes the book, her face freezes like she's lost in thought. "The weeks after she left the nursery were the worst with you. I thought I was gonna lose you so many times. Your lungs were so weak as it was, and yet you'd scream your little head off missing her so much. It was only after I thought to wrap you up in the blanket she'd used that you managed to calm down."

She turns around and starts rubbing my shoulders through my quilt.

"This one right here actually." Mom rubs the fabric of a small square of my quilt--the light pink square I always press my face to. Always.

"This was part of her baby blanket?" I ask.

She nods. "This one square is all I could save after the abuse you put it through." She sits down next to me and leans her head on my shoulder. "That's why I always use this blanket when you're sick. It seems to bring you back to life every time I think you're gonna leave me." I can hear the tears in her eyes. "Oh, listen to me, you must think I'm some nut now," she says, sitting herself upright.

"No, actually I don't. In fact, I think you might be right."

It's Mom's turn to look confused.

"Jada is connected to me in some way. I don't know how to tell you this without you going all nuts on me but Jada's the one who saved me during my asthma attack. And the one before that."

"I thought Ms. Philips found you on the road." She grabs my hand. "Start from the beginning, boy. And don't you leave anything out. You hear me?"

One look at her face and I know there will be no lying to her. Not after everything that's happened tonight.

Chapter 12

Jada

Kari stands hunched over the stove waiting for the tea water to boil. The way she slumps her back makes her seem frail, bent by some unseen burden. Somehow I know I've caused it. I just don't know how.

"What do you know about the day you were born?" Kari asks, clutching the tea pot.

My birth? *Why does she want to know about that?*

"You mean besides it being the worst day of my life?" I can't help but be sarcastic. She turns to look at me with a curious expression on her face. Of course she doesn't know about the tragedy that surrounded my birth, so I'm forced to say it. I wrap a hand around my leather band and squeeze hard, letting the pain surge through me before I can blurt out the truth.

"My mom died giving birth to me, and my dad hates me because of it."

Her reaction is typical. Her eyes grow wide; a small frown covers her face. I've made her uncomfortable. Good, maybe now we can drop the subject.

"Of course, that's all he would have told you. The rest probably seemed irrelevant after that." She sighs and turns back to the stove.

"What are you talking about? The rest of what?"

With great care, Kari picks up the teapot and brings it over to the table where she pours the steaming dark tea into two waiting cups. After taking a sip, she points to the news clipping.

"You've read this?"

I nod.

"Then you know most of it. I lost my best friend and the boy she loved that night, not because she had a crazy ex, but because she had found her Twin Flame."

Twin Flame. There is that phrase again. Mr. Harper mentioned it earlier this week too. What did finding soul mates have to do with anything? I consider saying as much but the way she looks, so deep in thought, I decide to just shut up and let her talk.

"For the record, I didn't believe in any of this crap when Naya told me about it either, but I was her friend so I listened. But then I witnessed it with my own eyes...the reality of it. I watched as my once timid friend, the one who always kept her eyes on the ground, turn into a crazed woman who was always searching for *his* eyes. Naya and Etash's love was the stuff they write books about, the kind of love no one really believes in, but wants to. They truly had found their other half in each other."

"And for a few brief moments, they were

happy. Hell, they'd even turned me into a believer; they had me thinking that someone was meant for me in this shit hole. Then...it ended. It took me a long time to get over their deaths. At first I blamed Seth, the ex, but then one day I figured it out. It's God. He doesn't want us to find love. He teases us with it. He'll give us tiny glimpses of it so we'll waste our lives looking to find it again. We do everything we can to remember it: write books, songs, plays, poems but we can't ever sustain it. Why? Because He doesn't want us to. He doesn't want to share His slice of heaven until He needs to. God is selfish. Just like the rest of us."

She picks up her tea again and takes a sip, watching my reaction. I don't know what she wants from me. She just sounds like a bitter old woman who got burned in the love department. Serves her right for falling in love in the first place.

"After they died," she goes on, "I felt numb. Depressed. I started wandering the halls of the hospital because I just couldn't go back to the dorms knowing that Naya wouldn't be coming back with me."

I'm having a really hard time understanding what any of this had to do with me, but I keep my mouth shut and let her speak.

"I was ready to scream at one point, but then I saw you."

I blink. "Me?"

She nods sagely. "Somehow I had managed to walk up to the nursery wing, and there you were, side by side with him."

"Him who?"

She gives me a tormented smile. "Tobias, of

course."

"Looking at the two of you, so calm and clearly enamored with each other, I just knew. I knew my friends had been reborn in you both."

I can't help but laugh.

"You think I'm your dead friend?"

Kari lets out an exasperated breath. She rubs her hands over her tired eyes. Her crows feet are barely visible, either from good genetics or a severe lack of smiling. I can't help but think it was the latter.

"Jada, I'm not going to sugar coat this. Stay away from Tobias, or you'll end up just like her!" She jabs her finger down at the image of her dead friend.

"You aren't making any sense!"

She walks over and holds onto my shoulders, and I do my best not to flinch. "I know this doesn't sound rational. You have no reason to listen to me. It's just a gut feeling I have. But I'm warning you that it's the same feeling I had before my best friend was murdered. Something bad is going to happen if you keep things going with Tobias." She lets out a deep breath in defeat. "I just don't know what."

Kari's eyes plead with such sincerity it's hard not to believe her.

"Please, can you just let me know if he was okay when you dropped him off," I beg.

"As long as you stay away from him, he will be." There is no vindictiveness in her eyes, just pain. I start to turn away from her sad eyes when she stops me.

"Tell me, Jada. What are the odds that I end up living next door to you? What are the odds that you were drawn to Etash's photo, the same way you're drawn to Tobias? Your souls are connected, just like theirs were, before they were killed." Her face is grim. "This isn't all just a big coincidence, and you know it."

I do my best to ignore the sense of dread that starts to pepper my skin. My gut tells me she's right, but my heart thinks only about Tobias. If I listen to her I'll have to stop seeing Tobias. And that is something I don't want to risk.

An unmistakable holler comes from outside. It's the one sound that can turn my blood cold.

"Jeanne!" The voice is terrifying, even from inside. It's my dad, calling out my mother's name. This is not good.

"I gotta go," I say. My skin is no doubt ashen with panic.

"Who is that yelling out there?" Kari goes to the window and pulls back a worn lace curtain.

His voice booms across the night sky again. "Jeanne! You better get your ass back in this house!"

Kari looks at me, confusion on her face. "Who is Jeanne?"

"My mother," I whisper, giving up the facade. "When he drinks, he sees her." Shame rattles through me as I clutch my leather binding.

Remember who you are.

Kari pulls the curtain closed then flicks off the light in the kitchen.

"What kind of drunk is he?" Kari asks me. I stare at her, blank faced. "Is he an angry drunk or will he just pass out?"

"Both."

Kari puts her hands on my shoulders again. I

hadn't realized I'd been shaking. She gives me a nod before she goes into the living room to dead bolt her door.

"You have no reason to be embarrassed," she says. "He's sick, honey. There isn't anything you can do about it, except protect yourself when it happens." She looks me in the eye. "Now do I have to dig out my BB gun or will he be okay out there on his own?"

We both listen in silence as he continues to yell.

"Jeanne? Why did you leave me again? Jeanne!"

I hate that I'm trembling so much. For all of my talk of being strong, he is the one person who can destroy my sanity in a flash.

"I should go." I swallow back some bile.

"Sorry, missy. You're *not* going back to that house tonight."

I sigh, not out of relief, but shame. "It's better to go back now than wait until morning. Trust me." I try to push past her, but her hands land firmly on my arms.

"Nope. No dice. You are not leaving this house." She gives me a stern look. "I'll use that BB gun on you if I need to."

That makes me laugh in spite of my fear. It's been years since he's been this bad. Moving back to the town where she died only seemed to only egg on his demons.

"I'm serious. You're staying whether you like it or not." She starts leading me down the hall and I actually let her. "I've got a spare room my sister uses sometimes. It's yours whenever you need it. You hear me?"

I nod at her because I can't speak. No one has ever been this nice to me.

She leaves me alone in the room after she gives me fresh sheets and an extra pillow from her room. When she closes the door behind me, I bury my head in the pillow and start to cry. With trembling fingers, I pull a quilt over my emotionally wrecked body and pray for sleep to take over. Outside I can only hear the sound of the last of the storm pass by. For now, that is enough. Tomorrow will bring a whole new storm, but right now, I have the night to gain my strength. I have a feeling I'm going to need it.

Tobias

I'm not sure how I thought Mom would take the news about Jada, but I certainly hadn't expected what I got: elation. She is positively tickled pink that we have 'found each other' again after all this time. She goes on and on about the role fate had played in all of this. It's actually starting to creep me out. Here is my mom, who is overjoyed with our meeting, and Kari, who is shouting about the dire consequences of our connection. I don't know what to think.

Eventually Mom shoves me off to bed, insisting that I still stay home tomorrow. I start to protest but realize I won't budge her tonight. She'll need to sleep on it, and so will I. But there is no way I'm staying home tomorrow. I need to see Jada. I need to know she's okay. Suddenly, her safety is more important than even breathing.

Relenting to a night of what is sure to be

fitful sleep, I wrap up in the quilt made up of Jada and smile. The image of her curled up, just like when we were infants, fills my thoughts. I can tell that she is sleeping. Safe. Somehow, I know this and that alone allows my body to do the same.

Chapter 13

Jada

I know it's a dream, but I don't want it to end. Tobias and I are in the woods, in our spot. It's raining. The cool drops seem to sizzle against my skin. He's looking at me with that half-grin of his and I know that he is about to kiss me. My heart thrums with the anticipation of his lips against mine. Inching closer, I feel his hand reach around my waist, closing what little gap there is between us. His long, lean fingers press deep against my back, hungry for contact. My breath comes in erratic bursts, desperate to taste him. Lightning flashes as he lowers his mouth to mine. When his lips finally crush into mine I realize something is wrong. His lips are hard.

Cold.

Possessive.

The hands that were once tender along my back now hurt. I can feel blood pooling under my flesh from his firm grasp. I push back from him, confused. Lightning flashes again.

Tobias is gone. Hawk holds me now. His eyes

are wild as he licks his lips and lowers his face to my ear.

"You can't hide from me, Jada. I'll hunt you down if you try. You're mine," he hisses.

I woke up screaming. My heart is in my throat and sweat is dripping down my face. His eyes--Hawk's icy eyes burn themselves into my mind.

"Jada?" Kari calls from behind the door.

Wiping the sweat off my head, I wrap myself up in the quilt tightly before I answer her.

"Come in," I croak. My voice shakes.

Kari pops her head in. "You okay, honey? I heard a scream." She's wearing an old, blue robe that looks incredibly soft.

"Yeah, sorry," I say. "Bad dream."

She purses her lips, unconvinced.

"Your dad called."

I bolt upright.

Dad.

"He asked if I'd seen you. I told him that I went over to your place before the storm got too bad to ask him for some help securing my windows, but since he was 'sleeping' you volunteered to help me. When the storm got worse, I wouldn't let you go out it in. Said we tried to call him but my battery was dead."

She comes to sit on the bed with me. Wow. That is a pretty good story.

"Did he believe you?"

She nods. "I think he did. Why would I lie?"

I bite my lip, hoping the cover will work.

"Does he leave for work before you leave for school?"

I glance at the clock beside the bed. "He's

already gone," I lie. I know what she's trying to do. She doesn't plan on letting me go back to the house while he's still there, but that's just delaying the inevitable.

"Good. Then I'll run down and make us some breakfast before school. How does that sound?"

How does that sound? It sounds too good to be true.

"Um, sure."

Kari stands up and leaves me alone in the room. When she's gone, I slide out of the covers and look out the window. Our house is in clear sight from here. Dad's bedroom curtains are closed, as always, but it's the kitchen I focus on. The house looks dark. To an outside observer it would look like he had already left for work, but I know better. He's down in the kitchen, waiting. Waiting for me.

The breakfast Kari makes feels warm going down my throat, but I don't taste it. My mind is trying to shut itself down.

At 6:30, I tell her I have to go home to get ready for school. I see the worry in her eyes, but she lets me go. It's not like she really has a choice. I have to go to school.

As I walk across our connecting yards, I feel my stomach churn. I barely make it to the front of the house before I throw up Kari's homemade breakfast.

With feet like lead, I climb up the front steps and open the door to accept my fate.

Chapter 14

Jada

Slipping into the darkness is the easy part. It's the coming out that blinds you.

Chapter 15

Jada

Even though my head is throbbing and feels thick, I can tell that nothing is broken. Taking a physical inventory, I can feel that my rib cage has taken the brunt of the blows. There may be one or two of them that are fractured, but the pain is tolerable. My arms are splotched with red but should fade by mid-morning. It will mean I'll need another long sleeve shirt in this damn humidity.

Standing, I walk over to my mirror. Except for the traitorous tears that have spilled and a bit of blood from a small crack in my lip, my face is fine. Nothing a little lip gloss can't cover.

Slipping into the tub, I carve out my 'A' without even looking. My fingers know their way by now.

The air count righted itself overnight so school isn't canceled. You'd think I'd want a day to rest with the pain I'm in, but I can't wait to get out of this house.

Once properly camouflaged to blend into the background, I start the walk to school. I'm annoyed that I have to walk slower because of the damn throbbing in my ribs. The only thing that pushes me on is knowing I'll get to see Tobias today. I have to know that he's okay.

At 8:45, I delicately perch myself in the entrance of the school and watch as students trickle in. The closer it gets to 9:00 and Tobias doesn't show, the more anxious I become.

Why is he not here yet? Did he get worse? Did he have to go to the hospital after all?

My eyes flick again to the road leading toward the school, but there are only a few clumps of girls straggling to the entrance. All around me people are pushing past me to get out of the wind and into the school. I stand firm in the door frame taking their passive aggressive hits, which makes my ribs scream, but I don't flinch. Not anymore.

Where is Tobias?

"Looking for me?" a voice whispers from behind me.

I jump a foot off the ground in surprise. I turn around slowly to see a concerned Hawk looking at me.

"Whoa. Sorry, I didn't mean to scare you." He lowers his shoulders to look me in the eyes. "Are you okay?"

"I'm fine," I say. "How is Tobias? Is he here? Is he okay?"

Hawk crinkles his eyebrows and cocks his head to the side.

"What do you mean? Why wouldn't he be okay?" His voice comes out slow.

"Wait, you didn't walk here with him today?" My head turns back to the road searching for him.

"No, we... had a disagreement. He doesn't want to speak to me right now."

Hawk turns my body to face him. He looks upset.

"I knew it. He's hurt, isn't he? I sensed something was wrong." He drags his fingers through his hair. "Tell me what you know!" he shouts, shaking me a bit.

I push his arms off me, annoyed. "He almost died last night. He got stuck in the storm."

A dark expression falls over Hawk's face. He grabs me around the waist and yanks me towards the underbelly of the stairwell. I have to bite my lip hard against the pain he's causing to my side.

"Tell me what happened," he orders. I'm shocked, not by his anger but by how scared he looks.

"He didn't tell you?"

Hawk sighs and tugs at his hair. "He won't talk to me." His body looks like its crumbling in on itself. He's really worried about Tobias.

I can't tell him the truth, that I just could sense Tobias out in the middle of a storm. I have a hard time believing it myself. So I tell as close to the truth as I can.

"He showed up at my house last night in the rain. He must not have made it home before the storm started. He could barely breathe. I took him to my neighbor's house. She has a car and she drove him home. He said he had meds there that would help but, now he's not here..." I bite my lip and walk back to the door praying he'll be walking down the road.

I feel Hawk follow beside me.

"He's okay. I'm gonna guess his mom kept

him home today. I would have felt it if it was bad."

I turn around to look at him. "Felt it?"

The first bell rings. The shuffle of feet above our heads begins to thrum loudly against the stairwell. "Meet me for lunch?" he says. "We need to talk."

"Um, okay," I blurt without thinking.

He gives me a small grin before he turns away and heads up the stairs.

My next two classes go from bad to worse as the minutes tick toward lunch. I can't concentrate on anything around me and nearly end up in the principal's office for not answering Mr. MacKamay's question about some ridiculous quote from *Romeo & Juliet*. Like I give a rat's ass about Romeo and Juliet right now!

Fortunately, I bite back my clipped reply and instead feign illness, which is not as hard to fake since my ribs are killing me. I get sent to the nurse's office to lie down.

Of course I don't actually make it to the nurse's office. I spend the last thirty minutes before lunch in the girl's bathroom splashing water on my face and downing pain meds so I don't walk funny anymore.

When the lunch bell finally rings, I slink out of the bathroom and disappear into the cafeteria. I'm only half aware of the food that is placed on my tray. I don't plan on eating it anyway, not today. I have a sneaking suspicion my digestive tract isn't going to work properly for the next few days. Pushing my food down the line, I wait patiently for the state mandated fluoride water. Can't have us getting cavities, now can we?

"Wow. That looks awful." A voice from behind

startles me. Like lightning, I tug my sleeves down thinking a bruise must be showing, but when I turn around, I find Hawk making faces at my lunch. Relief floods in.

"I've had worse," I throw back, doing my best to make a joke.

His smile softens. "I bet you have."

Flustered, I push my hair behind my ear, grab my tray and find the closest empty table. Hawk follows close behind me and slides himself into the chair right beside mine.

He leans back in the seat and gives me a look that I can't make out. It's almost like he's trying to get into my head.

"What?" I ask, unable to stop myself.

"Do I make you nervous?"

The question is so blatant and dead-on that I actually stutter out my reply. "Wh-what? No! Well, yes... um," I hang my head, embarrassed. "Maybe?"

I have just entered total loserville.

However, my answer seems to please him because he pulls his chair even closer to mine (if that is even possible) and drapes his arm across the back of my chair.

"Good," he whispers close to my ear. My face grows red. That one word sends a shiver up my spine, and it's impossible for me to tell if I like it or not.

Picking up my fork, I stab at what appears to be mashed potatoes. .

"So you were going to tell me about how you could feel how Tobias was okay." I say. Might as well cut to the chase.

He gives me a dark smile.

"It's just a gut feeling I get. I think because we were born on the same day, I'm connected to him somehow. When he's hurting, sometimes I can feel it too. Not every time, but a lot of the time. I felt something last night, but I thought it was just me feeling bad that we were fighting."

He stares solemnly at his tray.

"So, I told you one of my secrets, now you tell me what you're hiding."

I nearly choke on the small bite of potato I'd swallowed.

"I'm not hiding anything," I cough out, taking a quick peek at my arms to make sure.

Hawk sighs. "I know you're hiding something on your wrist. That strap of leather, although I'm sure is quite hip, isn't just for fashion."

Instantly, my hand is covering the cuff. He leans in close. "I can smell the blood, Jada." He points to his nose. "Tracker, remember?"

My heart starts to pick up. I have to think of something, fast. "It's a tattoo," I blurt. "Of something I'd like to forget."

Hawk's eyes narrow. He shakes his head. "You're a terrible liar."

Surprisingly annoyed at his cockiness, I yank at the cords and take off the cuff. I reach my hand across the table so my name throbs right in his face. Let him see the monster that I really am. Maybe now he'll leave me alone.

His face freezes as he takes in the scars. The 'A' is still crusted over with blood, but it is clear what I have done to myself.

He surprises me when rubs his thumb over the raised marks.

"They're beautiful," he whispers. The way he

says it, I almost believe him. Almost.

I try to say something, but I can't. Instead I rip my hand out of his grasp and I wrap my wrist up again, trying to process what he just said. My scars are not beautiful. They are morbid and twisted, just like I am.

We sit in silence for a few minutes. The hum of the lunch crowd is echoing in my ears. I'm listening hard to hear if anyone saw my arm, but it's clear that no one would have cared to look my way.

"We all have demons, Jada," Hawk says after a while. "I'll make you a deal. I won't judge you for yours if you won't judge me for mine."

I can't help but laugh at the ridiculousness of that statement. "What possible demons could you have? You're Mr. Greek God."

I expect him to laugh, or at least smile, but he doesn't. Instead, he looks like he's about to cry.

"I'm sorry. That was mean. It's just, it doesn't seem like you have any sort of outward problems that I can see."

He nods his head.

"Yeah. I fool a lot of people that way."

Intrigued, I reach out a hand and touch his arm. "What's your demon?"

He sits up straighter, takes my hand, and gives it a squeeze before he lets it go.

"I may have a tiny problem with my anger." He gives me a small smile before it fades. "I punched my best friend in the gut. My sick best friend. I mean, who does that?" He rubs his eyes with his hands. "I don't know what happened. One minute I was fine, the next, I was going crazy on him."

Although I'm not happy that he hit Tobias, it's clear that he's upset about doing it.

"Everyone loses it sometimes," I try.

"Yeah," he says, "Except with me, it's happening a lot more. Sometimes I feel like a monster."

The obvious pain in his voice disturbs me. I reach out and take one of his hands from his face.

His eyes open at my gesture.

"You're not a monster," I say.

"You don't know me well enough to say that," he says, slipping his hand out of mine.

Without another word, he pushes away from the table and walks away, leaving me wondering even more just who Hawk is.

Chapter 16

Tobias

Although she calls in every favor she can think of, Ma is unable to get her afternoon shift off from work, which means she'll have to go in after lunch. She makes me promise on a stack of Bibles that I will not leave my bed while she is gone. Since I don't believe in God, I have no problem lying to her.

I wait a good twenty minutes until after her ride picks her up before I dare to head to school. Triple checking my pockets, I confirm that I have my meds before I slip out the door and into the woods. I opt for the cover of the trees to take me to school. Sure, it will take longer, but if anyone sees me on the street, Ma might find out and I can't risk that. Besides, she has already told the school I won't be in, so it isn't like I can actually attend class. I just need to see her. Just once. Then I'll be able to breathe fully again.

At least that's the idea. It takes me almost an hour to make it to the school using the winding trail in the woods, but I'm also going slower on purpose. I can't risk pushing myself again.

When I finally make it to school, there is still about forty-five minutes left before they let out, so I take advantage of the time and rest my head against the cool earth. The sun above is shielded by the evergreens surrounding me. The gentle sounds of the wind and the birds in the trees fill the darkened woods, and I find myself closing my eyes to hear it better. As I listen, my breathing slows and my body relaxes. I feel myself floating in and out of sleep as I wait.

When my stomach clenches without warning, I know she is near. Sitting up, I hear the bell ring. I crouch down and peer out from the shadows. I'm suddenly aware that I'm holding the position Hawk has tried to teach me when he hunts. For some reason the idea disturbs me, so I stand up. That's when I see her.

Her golden hair swirls in the wind and I swear I catch her scent a moment later. She's calling someone's name over the sea of students. At first, I imagine that it's my name she's calling, but as she comes further down the stairs, I can hear who she really wants.

"Hawk! Wait up!" she yells. My eyes dart to find Hawk who turns to look at her but keeps walking. She starts pushing past those around her and is soon walking beside him.

As they move forward, so do I. I'm suddenly desperate to hear what they are talking about.

A few yards before my cover of woods disappears, they stop. Or rather Hawk makes her stop by grabbing her shoulder and turning him to her. My heart pounds in my chest waiting for her reaction; I wait for her to slug him or snap at him for touching her like that. What I don't expect, however, is what she actually does.

Jada

I've shouted his name at least a dozen times now. I know he hears me, which just makes me more determined to catch up to him. He's been avoiding me all afternoon, and I refuse to let him play mind games with me. He's trying to make me feel sorry for him, but it won't work. We've all got our baggage, and he needs to know I'm not going to fall for his trap.

"I know you can hear me, so stop being a dick and turn around!" I shout, causing a few girls nearby to giggle.

At that, Hawk stops. His shoulders square a moment before he spins around and grabs my arm so fast that I don't even have time to flinch.

"Stop following me," he hisses.

I rip my arm from his grip. "I'm not following you. I just want to talk to you."

"Why?"

It's my turn to stand up taller. "Because you need to know that I don't think you're a monster."

His nostrils flare at me. "You don't know anything about me."

He has me there.

"That's true, but just because you're moody doesn't mean that you're a horrible person. Trust me. I know horrible people, and you aren't one of them."

Those cool blue eyes of his lower to meet mine. Anger burns inside them.

"That's where you're wrong."

I step away from him, suddenly afraid.

"I smelled you in the woods that night. I had just gone out to do a little hunting, but then I caught your scent, and I was done for. Nothing else mattered to me then. I needed to find you. Hunt you down like an animal and make you mine. I didn't actually expect you to beg me to screw you. That was a bonus." He lowers his face to mine and whispers hot into my ear. "Now, tell me I'm not a monster."

But I can't. I can't say anything. I just stand there, shaking. It's not like I can accuse him of raping me because, technically, he didn't. I do remember begging him. I'm the monster, not him.

I don't know what I'm supposed to do or say, I just know I am so ashamed of myself that I have to get away from here, from him. So I do what I always do. I run. Pushing past him and his anger, I tear off down the road, ignoring the tears as they burn down my face.

Dirty. I just feel dirty. Used and tossed aside. And here I'd actually convinced myself that he cared about me, that I could learn to care for him. I am such a fool. My stupidity only makes me cry harder.

My sides are killing me, but I don't stop running. I can't. I just can't. If I stop running then I'll start thinking. Right now I don't want to think. I just want to go home, pop a few of Dad's pills and forget, just for a little bit. Just so I can find myself again. I'll be smarter about it this time. I'll only take one of his pills. Two, tops.

Once I finally reach my driveway, I slow my run to a jog until I finally collapse under the maple next to the house. My body hurts so much right now that it's hard to even breathe. Panting, I try to catch my breath and slow my heart rate down.

I stare up at the sun and feel it burn into my retinas. It makes my eyes water even harder than they already are. I let my tears wash away a fraction of the hurt.

I don't know how long I gaze at the sun. All I know is that it's been long enough to still my racing heart and dry the sweat from the nape of my neck. Part of me wonders if I could just stay here all night. I won't be missed.

That's when I hear the screen door slam from behind the tree.

"I know you're out here," Dad says. "You made a mess in my kitchen. You best get in here and clean it up." The mess I made? Right. The dishes that were broken when he was kicking me in the ribs. My mess.

I peek around the tree and see he is holding on tightly to a new bottle of vodka. A good third is already gone. Here we go again.

Like a robot, I pull my feet up to stand and start walking toward the house.

Tobias

I watch from the woods as Jada pushes past Hawk. He's upset her. Fury builds inside me for whatever he said, but I stay hidden. From the safety of the woods, I watch her tear off down the road. My legs try to follow after, but I force them still. Something inside me tells me to watch

Hawk.

His shoulders rock with anger or pain. It's hard to tell from here. I've never seen him so conflicted before. Eventually, he ducks into the woods about a mile ahead of where I'm hiding. He'll hunt himself out of whatever funk he's in.

Now that Hawk is gone, I turn my attention back to Jada. Emerging from my hiding spot, I start the long walk toward her house. I don't care if I'm seen anymore. All that matters now is if she's okay.

The dust kicks up as my feet travel down the road at a faster clip than I probably should, but my lungs feel fine. Stronger, actually, with each step I take closer to her. I can't help but think about what Hawk could have said to her to make her run all the way home. He better not have hurt her.

About five minutes away, I break into a run. Panic has filled my limbs and a desperate urge to get to Jada now consumes me, drags me along. Something bad is about to happen. Pushing harder against the ground, I run until I finally reach her driveway.

I slow to a jog when I see her outside. Relief floods over me as I look at her. Her blonde hair is shining in the afternoon sun as she pushes away from the huge maple tree. Panic returns. I can tell she's scared by the way her hand is pressed against the bark. Her long fingers are visibly trembling against the tree.

I slow down to a walk as I travel down her road trying to figure out her expression. It's a mix of fear and acceptance. It's only when I see what she is staring at that I understand.

There is a man half-standing and half-leaning on her porch. His unshaven face is slack but fierce as hell. There is no doubt about what she is terrified of: her own father. My stomach lurches.

"Hurry up!" the man yells. He doesn't appear to see me as he does his best to walk down the steps. He's drunk.

My eyes whip over to Jada who starts walking like she's on auto-pilot. Her face is blank of any emotion.

Snapping out of my shock, I run toward her.

"Jada!" I shout.

They both look up at me as I come barreling towards them. The father glares first at his daughter then back at me.

"Tobias?" I hear her whisper, but she stays rooted where she is.

When I get to them, I step in front of Jada and place my body in between her and her father. I bend down a bit to find her eyes.

"Don't go inside with him," I say. "He's drunk."

She gives me the saddest smile I've ever seen on a person. "I know. Which is why I need to go inside and you need to go home." She pats my hand gently. "I'll be fine. Go home. Please. I can handle this."

She pushes her shoulders back and tries to walk around me, but my hand flies out and tightens around her waist. I am not about to let her go in there with him.

I hear her father slur, "Say goodbye to your friend, Jada."

My nostrils flare when I feel her stiffen at the

sound of his voice.

"Goodbye, Tobias," she squeaks, trying to pull away again, but I don't let her. Instead, I take a step toward her father keeping my hand firmly around her waist.

"Mr. Williams, I don't believe we've met," I try. "I'm Tobias Garret. I go to school with your daughter."

He stumbles down the last step and comes nose to nose with me. The stench rolling off of him is almost unbearable.

"How nice." He spits at the ground. "School's over now. I need her to get her butt in the house, if that's all right with you."

"Actually, it's not all right with me," I say as calmly as I can. "Considering the state you're in."

Jada's hand balls into the back of my shirt, as though trying to pull me back.

Her dad blinks a few times then actually smiles at me. "What state is that?"

"Drunk before dusk," I say, my voice hard and flat. "Now, you're new here, so you may not know this, but drinking before sundown is illegal in this town."

His eyes narrow in such a way that I know damn well he knows the law.

"Is it now?"

"It is," I say, pushing Jada further behind me. "Now, my suggestion would be that you let Jada come home with me tonight so that I won't have to report to the authorities that I'd left a minor in the care of a drunk."

His face turns red before he spits again at the ground. "Well, ain't you the gentleman?"

Jada squeezes my hand, hard.

"That I am, sir." I pull her slowly down her driveway, keeping my eyes on her father. "I'll see that she gets to school in the morning. You have a good evening."

Her dad's mouth starts to open but then stops. His eyes burn into his daughter and I hate that. I turn her around and push her forward. I never want her to endure that gaze again.

Jada's body has gone limp as I shove her forward. It's almost like she doesn't dare leave, which makes me even more determined to get her out of here.

Chapter 17

Jada

As I walk down the road that leads me away from my house, I know my future is hanging in the balance. I haven't openly defied my father like this in years. I still have the fake tooth to prove it.

I was fifteen. There was a dance at school that I had asked to go to with some friends I'd managed to make. Of course he'd said no, but I snuck out and went anyway. He was waiting for me when I tried to crawl back in through my window. It scared the hell out of me, seeing him sitting in the corner of my room, empty bottle at his side.

He raged on and on about what a tramp I'd turned into. Told me how my mother would have been so ashamed of me. I was a disgrace to her memory.

That was the first night he had polished off an entire bottle of vodka in one sitting. It was also the first night he'd ever hit me. He used the bottle first against my rib cage, but when I stood up, he moved up to my face. All I remember is waking up in a pool of blood and missing my bottom canine.

Last year, when he 'quit' drinking, I thought we'd said goodbye to days like that. Sure, we'd just gone from physical abuse to flat out ignoring me, but at least that didn't leave so many visible marks.

As Tobias drags me away I can't help but think that if I go home right now I might get myself out of the worst of it, but if I continue on with Tobias, I'll be sealing my fate for sure.

Glancing behind me, my house disappears in the distance. I half expect my dad to come barreling down the road after me, but then that would mean he cared about me on some small level, and--he just doesn't.

I turn to look up at Tobias. His face is troubled and his lips are drawn firmly together. He's refused to let my hand go since he took hold of it earlier, and I don't try to take it away. Instead, I just I hold on tight and let him lead me away from reality, if only for tonight.

Several minutes pass in silence before Tobias opens his mouth but then closes it. I know he wants to ask about my dad, but I can't admit the truth, even when he's seen a glimpse of it. Denial is a powerful thing.

After a few minutes he tries again. "Do you want to talk about it?"

I tighten my grip on his hand. "Not really."

He nods. "Okay then."

As we approach his house, he slows us down to a crawl.

"My mom's gonna be pissed at me," he says. "I took off without permission. Again." He gives me a sheepish smile.

"I should go then," I say automatically. "I don't want to get you into more trouble..." I stop walking and release his hand. Coldness washes over me. I should have known I can't escape my dad.

Tobias grabs my hand back and his warmth returns. My skin prickles. "You're not going back there tonight." He looks me dead in the eyes. "You got it?"

I nod and allow him to lead me to his porch. As he climbs the steps, he groans. There's a note stuck to the door.

"It's from my mom. She called Kari. They're out looking for me."

He digs out his e-portal to send word that he's home. He unlocks the old wood door, pushing against it with a large heave. Once inside he asks, "How about you help me make some dinner. That might help get me out of the mound of shit I've dug myself into."

I laugh in spite of my nerves.

"I'm a horrid cook, but sure."

He leads me into the kitchen, which is small like mine, but infinitely brighter, and way more inviting. Their house is like something out of an e-mag. The walls are a pale yellow that burn bright against the afternoon sky. There is delicate daisy-tile pattern that runs along the edge of the counter-tops, oozing even more cheerfulness.

"We can start with these," Tobias suggests, pulling out a large sack from under the sink. He plunks the worn canvas bag down with a thud. Opening the sack, he dumps out the contents.

"Are those what I think they are?"

He smiles, but it's an embarrassed smile.

"Um, yeah. They're potatoes."

"*Real* potatoes?" There haven't been real potatoes in the states for years now, not since the potato bugs wiped them out.

"Yeah," he laughs, grabbing one of the spuds and rolling it across the table to me. I pick up the thing and just look at it. It's got these strange little nubs poking out of it. "Don't worry, we cut those off," Tobias says, sensing my hesitation.

I flush red. "Sorry, I just never had to peel one, even before the contamination. We've always done boxed. Pretty pathetic, huh?"

Tobias shakes his head and smiles. "No, not really. I wish we did. It would save me a lot of work. Ma and I grow these in the basement, so we never got infected ones. Not many people would bother to take the time to do that when boxed is so much cheaper."

"But I'm sure these taste better," I say, wagging the potato at him.

"That they do."

We spend the next few minute cutting off the roots and chopping them into small bits. The quietness that surrounds us as we cut and peel the potatoes is soothing and strangely therapeutic. As they boil, Tobias and I head into the living room. He sits in an old rocker and I perch on the end of the sofa, not sure what to say.

"So, you and Hawk had a fight?" Tobias coughs out after a moment.

"What?" I ask.

Tobias frowns at me. "I saw you talking to him today. At school."

"You were there? I didn't see you." I don't admit that I had been looking for him.

"After my mom left for work, I snuck out. I needed to get out of the house." He shifts in his seat, clearly uncomfortable. "When you took off, I assumed you two had a fight. I followed after you to make sure you were okay. I'm glad I did."

I pull my legs up onto the couch, hugging them. "I don't want to talk about Hawk."

Thankfully, Tobias nods. "Okay. What do you want to talk about?"

The way he's leaning in the chair, his sexy curls almost reaching his eyes, his soft lips looking deadly kissable--well, I can't help myself. "I don't want to talk at all," I say in a voice huskier than I knew I had.

Without thinking, I'm on my feet. A second later I'm straddling him on the rocker, caging his body beneath mine. His body hardens underneath me, confirming my suspicions about how he thinks of me. Desire floods over me as he lets out a small moan. His hands tentatively encircle my hips before they get bold and pull me closer.

I lick my lips in anticipation as my fingers curl into the back of his hair, holding on tight. His skin is electric against mine.

Our lips inch closer; the heat of his breath makes me dizzy. Our noses brush against each other so tenderly that it makes me ache with need. His fingers dig in harder against my hips pulling me into a deep embrace. Our lips are seconds away from connection. My body aches with anticipation.

"Tobias Daniel Garret!" a voice booms from behind us.

I feel myself whimper as Tobias pushes me off him, cursing under his breath. I do my best to straighten my clothes and push down my hair, but the embarrassment is too thick to cover.

"Ma, you're back," Tobias says, crossing his legs, not quite able to stand up yet.

"Where the hell have you been?" she asks in a slow and measured voice. "And who is this?" Her arms fold across her chest.

"I went for walk. I was bored. This is Jada. Happy now?"

Her eyes dart back to me. Her mouth opens, as though in shock, then a second later her hands are crossed back over her chest. She looks back at Tobias.

"We need to talk. Now." She turns around and walks into the kitchen.

"I'll wait outside," I say, knowing he'll need privacy. No one likes getting yelled at in public, that much I know.

He gives me a sheepish smile and takes my hand. Heat surges into me. "Thanks. I won't be long." He looks into the kitchen and then back at me. "I hope." Reluctantly, he lets my hand drop and goes to find his mother.

As soon as he is in the kitchen, I head outside and do what I should have done earlier. I slide down the stairs and head back home. It's time for me to grow up and take my punishment, just like Tobias is doing.

Tobias

Pushing through the kitchen door, I start thinking about what my defense will be.

"Ma, before you start in on me–"

"Are you cooking potatoes?" Ma asks before I can finish my thought.

"Yeah. Jada and I thought we'd make shepherd's pie for dinner."

She pursed her lips. "She's staying for dinner?"

Clearing my throat, I try to find my courage. "Actually, I've told her she could stay the night."

"Tobias!" she shouts.

I walk closer to Mom, trying to shush her. The last thing I want is for Jada to overhear us. She already feels guilty for coming, and I don't want her to change her mind.

"Her dad was drunk, Ma, and he looks like a mean one. I can't let her stay there tonight." *Or ever again.*

Mom gives a worried look towards the living room but nods. "All right. She can stay, but she's sleeping on the couch. And you are going back up to your room and plugging yourself back in."

"I'm fine, Ma," I say, but she lifts a finger at me.

"She stays only if you take your medicine until dinner time. I'll see that Jada is taken care of. Don't you worry. She and I will get along all right. I'll have her help me finish dinner and then I'll call you down. Deal?"

"But... " I try.

She gives me a stern, raised eyebrow.

"Fine," I say, giving in and dragging my feet

up the stairs.

As I climb the stairs the days events of the day start to wear on me, and I feel the strain it's put on my lungs. I guess a nap wouldn't hurt, and neither would Ma getting to know Jada. Grunting, I force myself into my room, trying to push away the knot that is forming in my stomach.

Jada

I don't remember the walk back to my house. It's like my brain shut off, which is probably for the best.

My only shot at getting out of a beating tonight is if he's passed out, which isn't out of the question. It's that hope that allows me the courage to open my front door.

However, when I walk into the kitchen, he's there. He's sitting at the table with his feet up, the bottle of vodka still lodged tight in his hand. His eyes are completely bloodshot and murderous when he sees me.

"Well, well, well. Look who decided to come crawling back," he taunts, standing up and taking a swig.

"I'm sorry," I blurt out, doing my best to hide my shaking limbs. He hates to see weakness.

"No. You're not sorry. But you're gonna be."

As he stumbles over to me, I try to shut down my senses. I have to find a place to escape inside my mind until it's over. The first blow comes before I'm ready. Even though my eyes are closed, I know what I've been hit with. The dull thud of the vodka bottle breaking against the kitchen table is unmistakable. A second later my skin is torn open. The warmth of my own blood trickles down my face as pain sears from the corner of my left eye down to my jaw. I feel my mouth open up to scream. But no sound comes, muted after years of keeping the punishments private.

I stumble to the ground and reach for my face not daring to open my eyes, terrified by what I'll see. He went for the face, which means he doesn't care what the outcome will be. I was to be taught a lesson, one he wanted to make sure I'll never be allowed to forget.

With one hand pressed against my face to hold my skin together, I inch away from him, only stopping when I reach the kitchen wall. A second slash comes at me. This time it's my shoulder.

"Damn you, Jeanne!" my father screams my mother's name at me. "Why did you have to leave me?"

I try to open my eyes, but only the right one will budge. The left is either swollen shut or is gone for good.

Dad sinks down to his knees beside me. He grabs my torn face in his hands, seemingly unaware of the pain he is causing by touching the open flesh.

The look on his face terrifies me. He's not here. His mind is gone, off somewhere else. His eyes are glassed over with tears. "I chose you, Jeanne, not her!" he weeps. "I told God to save you!"

He raises the bottle again, and I know that this will be the blow that kills me.

"I'm ready," I whisper to the heavens, happy

for the chance to finally rest.

"Let her go!"

I rip my lids open. Intense pain sears my left eye. I am able to make out Hawk's body standing the kitchen door. His drawn arrow is aiming right at my father.

I try to tell him to stop, that it's too late to save me, but my voice comes out garbled. My dad yells something I can't make out, and then a moment later an arrow is lodged inside my dad's chest.

His agonized scream is the last thing I hear before the lights go out.

Chapter 18

Tobias

"Hawk! What did you do?" I scream, pushing him out of the way. I rush to Jada needing to check on her first.

"You told me to shoot!"

"I meant in the leg or something, not a kill shot!"

He lowers the bow as I kneel down and check for Jada's pulse. As soon as I touch her skin, I know she's alive. Her flesh, although badly mutilated, is like fire against my cool fingers. Her heart is thrumming wildly, but with the amount of blood she's losing, it won't be long before she could be in serious jeopardy. I can't let that happen.

"Okay, I think she's just passed out, but we need to cover her wounds and get her to a hospital fast. I'll take care of her, you check on her dad."

Hawk doesn't move. He just stands there, bow in hand, staring at the man he most likely just killed.

"Hawk, look, I know you're freaking out. I am, too. But we need to try and save them, okay? I can't do this alone. I need your help."

"I didn't mean to hurt him," he whispers. "I just wanted him to stop hurting her." A tear runs down his face. I have never seen Hawk cry.

Standing, I walk over to him and put my hands on his shoulders, shaking him a bit so he'll look at me.

"You acted on instinct. No one will blame you for that. But right now we need to focus on stopping the bleeding, okay?"

"I can't..." He backs away from Mr. William's limp body.

"Fine. I'll check on him, while you get her bandaged up." I pull out my e-portal and hit the emergency button. It will instantly hone in on my GPS. They should be here within a few minutes. It isn't like me to be the one in control. I am used to taking orders, not giving them.

Hawk nods slowly. He begins to rummage around the kitchen looking for dishcloths to try and stop Jada's bleeding.

I sink down to the ground to take a closer look at the spot where the arrow pierced him. Unfortunately for Mr. Williams, Hawk's a good shot. He slipped the arrow right in between his ribs, making a clean hit to either his heart or his lung. Either way, unless the ambulance gets here soon, he won't make it. The ambulance...They'll see the bow. They'll know how he died.

"We have to remove the arrow," I whisper.

Hawk stops wrapping up Jada and looks at me.

"If you take the arrow out, he'll bleed out."

I know he's right. If all of my time hunting with Hawk has taught me anything, it is how badly an animal bleeds once you remove the head of the arrow. After all, they are designed to go in, not out.

"Hawk, we have to get it out before the paramedics come."

"No, man. I think we should wait."

He doesn't understand, so I do my best to remain calm. "Hawk, what do you think the paramedics will say if they find an arrow head that you carved, that's probably covered with your prints, inside his chest?"

His eyes grow wide in understanding as they flick between Jada and her father, then back at me. He grows rigid—scared. It's the first time I've ever seen him terrified of anything. The reality of what had just happened is setting in.

Seeing his face drain of color, I can't help but feel guilty. This whole thing is my fault. I forced him to come here tonight. When Ma came up to tell me that Jada had gone back to her fathers, I went nuts. While Ma called the cops, I took off after her. I knew I wouldn't be strong enough to confront her dad on my own, though, which is why I got Hawk and his bow to join me. The weapon was supposed to just be for show: a bluff. Just a way to get her away from her dad. *How had things gone so wrong?*

One thing is clear: there is no way Hawk is taking the fall for something I orchestrated. Thinking fast, I scan the room looking for something sharp. The vodka bottle. It will be perfect. Still dripping with Jada's blood, I grab the bottle and bring it over to Mr. Williams.

"What the hell are you doing?" Hawk screams at me. He knocks the bottle out of my hand. As it falls, it takes a huge gouge out of my arm. I let out a scream of my own.

"Damn it, Hawk! I'm trying to save your ass! This has to look like this was a struggle and not like you shot him with a bow and arrow at close point range! Unless you want to go to prison for the next five to ten years! It has to look like an accident. We have to remove the arrow and something needs to take its place as the weapon."

"But you could kill him!"

I look down at the limp body on the ground, surprised to find no remorse for the man lying there.

"He deserves to die after what he's done to her."

The blood from my arm starts to seep in between my fingers and drip onto the tile. Looking at it dot the floor makes my head feel light. There seems to be an awful lot of blood for such a small cut. Blinking my eyes back into focus, I turn back to Mr. Williams and raise my hand, but I can't seem to do what needs to be done.

"Let me do this!" Hawk grunts. "You always were a pansy around blood."

I feel the bottle slip from my hands before Hawk pushes me to the ground. My eyes close against the sound Mr. Williams' screams of agony as Hawk removes the arrow. The last gurgle of breath escapes her father's lips when Hawk lodges the broken bottle where the arrow had been.

The brutality of what he just did makes me want to hurl. It takes me a moment to regain my thoughts.

"Hawk!" I yell. "You've got to get out of here."

His lips twitch. "I won't let you take the blame for this."

My shoulders slump. "Why not? I'm the one who told you to shoot."

"But I'm the one who killed him!"

I close my eyes against the throb in my arm and the burn that's starting up in my lungs.

"Hawk," I say slowly. "You and I both know I won't be around much longer. I'm not letting you ruin your life when mine is all but used up." His face contorts. Sirens start to wail in the distance. "Go. Now. For me."

The hesitation is in his eyes, but after a moment his resolve fades and he bolts out the door, giving me one last sidewards glance as he leaves.

Suddenly terribly winded, I limp over to Jada and cradle her in my good arm. Her body is like Jell-O under me, but I can still see her chest rising and falling. She'll be okay. She has to be.

Looking down at her angelic face, I find myself unable to resist. I brush my nose against the side of her face. She's warm. Alive. With the last of my strength I lower my lips to hers. As they touch, a thousand images flash across my eyes: a vodka bottle, pills--lots and lots of pills--a girl crying in agony, a bloody belt and a shotgun going off.

I rip my lips off Jada's in horror.

What the hell was that?

The shock of what I'd just seen combined with the strain of the night leaves my lungs burning for air. A coughing fit begins, making

Jada bounce wildly in my arms, but I refuse to let her go. I need my inhaler which is sitting in my pants pocket. I try to shift Jada off of me to fish it out but I can't do it with just one arm, and the other one is throbbing so badly that I can't think straight.

Stars start to dance across my eyes. I try to blink them away, but they just keep coming. Eventually, the stars win and I can't even manage to open my lids back up.

Sirens get louder in some corner of my mind. Help is coming. I allow my eyes to close against the rush of noise inside my head.

Jada

Bleach. The smell of it stings my nose and brings me back into the world I thought I escaped. A steady beeping sound comes from my right. I try to open my eyes, but only the right will budge. My hands try to feel for the reason why but only my left one will move without pain. My limited sight reveals that a sling is clasped tight to my torso, imprisoning my right arm, while an IV hinders my left arm.

The room is dark, illuminated only by a million beeping machines. Along the edge of my bed, I find the nurses' call button which I somehow manage to press with my limited motion.

As I wait, my fingers find the cause of what's obscuring my vision. The whole left side of my face feels like it is covered in gauze, and it hurts. A lot. A groan escapes my lips as I try to sit up.

"Easy now," a voice says entering the room. It's a voice I recognize.

"Ms. Garret?" I croak. I'm surprised by how strange my voice sounds.

"Call me Brenda, honey." Brenda checks my machines before she looks at me. Her nostrils flare a bit, angered by what she sees. Is she angry at me? My father? Her son? Hawk?

"What are you doing here?"

She smiled. "I work here, darling. You've been out for almost three weeks now. You were starting to get us worried."

Three weeks?

"Tobias' doctors won't let him come visit you since his lungs are still so weak. He's made me come here every day to check on you, even the days I'm not on duty." She smiles softly at me. "I think that boy is smitten with you."

"My father, is he..."

Brenda sits down at the foot of the bed and folds her hands. "I'm sorry, honey. He didn't make it."

My eyes fill with tears but only one eye can release them.

"What happened?"

She sighs. "I was hoping you could tell me. Tobias won't say a word."

"It was Hawk..."

She nods. "We know. He confessed before..." She drops her head to the floor.

"Before what?"

When she raises her head, she looks terribly disturbed. "Before they took him to prison."

"What?"

"His lawyers think he's gonna end up with

three years for involuntary manslaughter."

I try to swallow, but my throat is too tight. *Three years.*

"But he was just trying to protect me..."

"I know that, honey, but he still killed a man with an illegal weapon. He'll be lucky to get off with that."

"This is all my fault. If I hadn't left your house...if I had just stayed where I was, none of this would have happened." The truth of the situation begins pressing down on me. If I had just done what Tobias asked me to do and stayed away from my father when he was out of control, none of this would have happened. The guilt is overwhelming. I can actually feel the color draining out of me.

"You look a little pale. How is the pain? I wish I could give you more," she sighs, "but because of your condition, it would be risky."

"My condition?"

Brenda cocks her head then squeezed my hand. "Oh honey, I thought you knew. The way Tobias talked..." She presses her lips into a huge smile. "Jada, honey, you're gonna be a mamma."

My heart stops.

"What? No--that's impossible..."

She smiles at me. "The docs were a little surprised, too. When they did an ultrasound to check for more internal bleeding last week, they found your baby's heartbeat instead. Don't you worry, honey, your baby is just fine. But because of that I can't give you anything stronger than acetaminophen."

"But," I whisper. "I've never..."

Hawk.

That night in the woods.

My throat tightens and tears begin to flow down my face without consent.

Brenda sits beside me and wipes them away.

"Hush now, honey. Don't you cry. Tobias is gonna be a wonderful daddy. He's gonna take care of you both."

Her figure has blurred behind the tears. "Tobias... knows?" I squeak.

"He does, honey. And he's so happy."

I do my best to swallow the lump lodged in my throat. Tobias knows I'm pregnant with Hawk's baby, so why is he trying to pretend it's his?

"Now you go on and rest. I'm gonna go find your doctor. He's gonna want to run some tests on you now that you're awake."

I nod even though I don't feel myself do it. My hand drifts over to my belly.

"Ms. Garret?"

She stops at the door.

"Yes, darling?"

"How bad is my face?" I move my hand over to my bandaged face and search her two perfect eyes for the truth.

Her lips form a thin line; I know she'll be honest. "The doc says you won't lose your eye."

I close my eye, waiting for the rest. "But..."

Brenda exhales loudly. "But there will be a scar."

My lips quiver as I try to hold back tears. "I want to see."

"I don't think that's--"

"If you won't help me, I'll do it myself."

Determined, I start clawing at the gauze. I

need to see what I've become.

"All right, stop it now. Don't go ripping your stitches open! Let me help." She bats my hands away and starts to slowly undo the tape. My face throbs as she pulls it away from my skin. The gauze needs to be peeled off slowly so it doesn't break the new skin growing below. It feels like each piece she removes takes a bit of who I used to be away.

The left side of my face stings. Pulses of pain rocket throughout my head, giving me an instant migraine. From my good eye I can see the edge of my cheek, which I know will be bruised beyond recognition.

Brenda walks over to one of the cabinets and returns with a hand mirror. "It's still pretty swollen," Brenda warns. "And they haven't done any plastic surgery yet, so--"

"Give me the mirror."

Reluctantly, she hands a small mirror to me. Holding my breath, I look.

My left eye is completely swollen shut. A mix of purples and yellows line the side of my face. They are colors to which I've grown accustomed, just not on my face. Experience tells me that the swelling will go down and my true color will return, but it's the jagged line of black stitches running from the edge of my eyebrow down the side of my face and along my jaw line that will never fade. This horrid scar will never disappear. It will remain as a constant reminder of what my own father had done to me. A permanent reminder of how much he'd hated me, of how he didn't love me.

How could I ever be a mother being as messed

up as I am?

Clutching on tight to the mirror I feel it snap under the pressure I'm putting on it. It's plastic, not glass, but the edges will still be sharp. It will do just fine. I curl myself up into a ball and weep, waiting for Ms. Garret to leave me in peace so I can fix this.

Chapter 19

Tobias

The robotic hiss of the nebulizer attached to my face may be keeping me alive, but it's also keeping me awake. For weeks now, I've been chained to this stupid machine, making it impossible for me to go and check on Jada. Since that last night in her house, I've gone downhill fast. Each day it gets harder to just catch my breath.

Doc said because of all the damage I have done to my lungs, I'll probably be on this damn thing for the rest of my life, unless I get a lung transplant. That's not happening any time soon. In the meantime, Mom has ordered a portable nebulizer, but it hasn't come in yet and the wait is killing me.

After everything that happened these last few weeks, I've barely been able to keep anything down. I've lost about ten pounds, which isn't good when you're as sick as I am. Between Jada being in a coma and Hawk being thrown in jail, it's all been too much to process.

Every day that passes without seeing Jada, I grow more and more restless, weaker, somehow. The romantic in me wants to believe that if I could just see her, I will be healed. But the realist in me knows better.

I toss and turn in my bed unable to rest. Out of the blue, my heart squeezes. The hairs rise on my arm.

Jada.

Bolting upright, I hear the front door shut. Ma's home. I glance at the clock. 2:15am. Her shift should have been over hours ago. The only time she's ever late is if someone has crashed, or worse. Panic ensues.

"Mom!" I shout down the stairs. "Mom!"

I hear her drop her bag on the table before she comes thundering up the stairs.

"Tobias? What is it, honey? I'm coming!"

She swings open my door, worry etched on her forehead. "What is it? What's wrong?" she pants.

"I'm fine," I say coughing. "What's wrong with Jada?" I rip off my mask.

Mom rushes to my side and shoves it back over my face. "You leave that on, mister, or I won't tell you anything!"

I know she's full of shit, but I don't want to risk it. I need to know what's going on.

"Fine," I mumble through the plastic.

She moves a chair next to the bed. The legs scrape against the floor, making my head hurt. She lets herself fall into the rocker. It feels like an eternity as she takes a couple of breaths. She wipes the sweat from her forehead with the back of her hand before she finally speaks.

"She's awake."

She's awake. The words resonate in my head over and over: she's awake. My heart fills at just the thought of her.

Her being awake is all the motivation I need. I rip off the covers and toss the mask to the floor.

"Tobias! Get back in that bed!"

"Ma, if she's awake, I have to go see her!" Why doesn't she understand that? Doesn't she see how miserable I've been?

She puts her hand softly on my shoulder lowering me down again.

"Yes, you do; but not until the portable nebulizer comes in. It should be here in the morning. Maybe by then she'll be ready for company." Mom looks out the darkened window.

"What are you not telling me?" I ask, taking a puff off my nebulizer.

Her face pinches.

"I told her about the baby...I thought she knew. The way you talked about her pregnancy..."

I stiffen. I never told Ma the baby was mine. She just assumed. Of course, I didn't correct her either. And now Jada not only knows she was pregnant, but that I'm claiming it as mine. She must be furious with me.

Mom squeeze my hand. "I'm sorry she found out that way honey. I feel just awful. Oh Lord, forgive me, but I think I went and made things worse."

Worse? "What did you do, Ma?"

She buries her head in her hands. Oh, this is going to be bad.

"Tobias, it wasn't my fault. I tried to stop her."

"What did you do?"

"I let her see her face."

"What?" I rip off the mask and stand up.

"She was tearing at the bandages, Tobias! I was afraid she'd pull out the stitches or make it worse, so--I let her see." A tear runs down my mother's face.

My skin goes numb. I remember very clearly what her father had done to her. And now so would she.

Ma grabs my hand. "Tomorrow. You'll see her tomorrow. Then you can bring her back."

I blink, confused. "Bring her back? From where? I thought you said she woke up?"

Ma nods. "Her body woke up but once she saw her face, Tobias, her spirit went back to sleep." She sighs. "She curled herself up into the fetal position and hasn't budged since. I sat with her for two hours, trying to get her to unwind herself but...she's checked out, Tobias. And I think you might be the only one who can bring her back."

My hand slips out of hers and suddenly, I can feel it, Feel Jada's despair. She feels like her own child will never love her because of her scar. She thinks she's a monster. A toxic ache seeps into my veins. This can't wait for tomorrow. She has given up. I need to get to her now.

There is only one problem: Ma.

That means I'll have to give the performance of my life to get her to go to sleep so I can slip out.

"I hate that I can't see her," I say, lying down, feigning defeat.

"I know, baby, but your lungs are just too weak to take the trip in now. Once the nebulizer arrives, I promise we'll take a cab and see her. Okay?" She leans over me and kisses my head.

"Okay," I sigh, for effect.

Ma stands up and rubs her eyes.

"I'm gonna hop in the shower before I crash. Are you sure you're okay?" She touches my forehead, searching for a fever that's never there.

When she's satisfied that I'm normal, I turn off my bedside light and yawn a weak, "I'm just tired, Mom."

"Me too." She gives me a quick kiss on the head and then walks over to the door. "I'll be up in a few hours to get you your meds. Try and get some rest."

"You too."

She nods then walks out, turning off my overhead light.

As soon as the door closes, I sit up in bed and wait. A few minutes later, the sound of water running confirms she's in the shower. I pull back the covers and let my bare feet hang over the bed. Keeping the mask on for as long as I can, I tear off my sweatpants, grab a pair of jeans from off the floor, throw my shoes on and then stop to listen again. The water is still running. Good.

I stuff my inhaler into my pocket, take one last inhalation of medicated air and then take the mask off, letting its tell tale hum continue on without me.

My lungs tense at the withdrawal of the healing mist, but I'm too stubborn to give up before I even begin. Tip-toeing down the stairs, I slip out the back door and grab my old bicycle. I haven't ridden it in years, but I know I won't be able to walk all the way to the hospital, not even under the best of conditions.

Using all my strength, I painstakingly push it slow out of the driveway. I can't risk Mom hearing me out here. Once I clear the house I have to take a few drags off my inhaler before I can even get on the bike. It's amazing how weak I've become since getting out of the hospital. This is, by far, the worst I've ever felt. For the first time since being told my lungs were working on borrowed time it actually felt like they were. My brain screams for me to go back to the nebulizer, but my feet push me forward as Jada pulls me to her.

Straining, I lift my leg over the bike and push down on the peddle. I'm amazed at how hard it is to get it going. Thankfully, the road leading to the hospital is on a slight hill so I'm able to coast a majority of the way.

As I get closer to the hospital, I find that it is starting to get a little easier to breathe. Maybe it's the cold air making the oxygen easier to reach my lungs.

It's only when I step inside the hospital, however, that I realize it's not the cold. Inside, my breath comes easy and swift. The pain in my lungs has receded and my muscles actually feel thick and strong. Intuitively, I know it's because of Jada. She's making me stronger. That has to be it. I went downhill the moment they took me away from her, just as she started to slip downward without me near her. Just like when we were babies.

The way my body feels is all the proof I need. We *have* to be together. It is suddenly the clearest thing I've ever known. It fills me with such intense happiness that I actually start to tear up.

Without warning, the scar on I have on my arm from where the bottle sliced me that night starts to burn as though it's being cut open again. Tearing at my sleeve, I pull back my shirt, but the scar isn't bleeding at all. In fact, it's been healing nicely. The pain comes again, hot and fast, like a bolt of lightning.

Jada!

"Someone help!" I shout, running towards her room. A few nurses turn to look at me before they drop their tablets and follow behind me.

"Sir, what's wrong?" one of them shouts.

"It's Jada Williams! Room 111. She's hurt!" My heart is throbbing in my chest. *I have to get to her!*

Running down the hall to her room, I slide to a stop. I push against the door, but it doesn't budge. I shove it again, but it only opens a fraction of an inch. Something heavy is lodged against it from the other side.

"Jada! Open the door!" I scream into the darkness.

My heart is pounding in my ears as I press against the door to listen.

"Go away. You're too late anyway," comes Jada's defeated whisper.

No. Please, God, no.

Chapter 20

Jada

It began innocently enough. Once Ms. Garret finally left, I pushed the bed against the door and started work on carving the final 'A' into my arm. But when my fingers started over and began carving a new letter over my 'J,' I kinda flipped out.

Instead of my own name staring back at me, I have carved a whole new name into my flesh.

Naya.

The letters of my name have all but vanished under the new carving. Blood pours out of the gashes, but I don't feel a thing. All I can hear is Naya's name chanting over and over in my mind, the name of some dead girl I've never even met.

This is too much. Not only am I carrying the child of the man who murdered my father, but I'm also horribly disfigured and hearing things.

This has got to stop, and I have to be the one to stop it.

Grabbing hold of the ragged edge of the

shard of plastic, I move my hand away from its possessed carving. My hand shakes a bit while I gather my courage.

When I hear that cursed name inside my head again, I slide the broken edge fast across my wrist, hoping to finally silence it.

That's when a new pain begins.

At first, my arms feel like they are on fire. It's like liquid hot lava cascading down my flesh. I sink my teeth into the hospital pillow to muffle my screams. Eventually, my limbs start to turn cold. The chill travels down my arms first, putting out the fire, then it travels strangely into my legs. That's when my head starts to spin. I close my eye against the mounting pressure on my chest. It almost feels like I'm floating. Lying down onto the floor, I see a bright light forming above me. It's so beautiful.

The final strike to my heart is the far off sound of Tobias. He's too far away to actually reach me though.

Looking down at my arm, I can see the blood, so dark it's almost black. It seeps into the edges of my hospital gown slowly crawling up the fibers. It's fascinating to watch.

"Jada!"

There it is again. Oh, if only he were really here. But then, it's too late for dreams. It's too late for me. How sad is it that he would be the only thing I would miss? I start to cry, devastated that he isn't the Angel that is starting to call me home.

Tobias

"Jada!" *Don't you dare die on me*. I make a running dive for the door and slam into it, hard. It opens a few more inches. With the help of the nurse, we're able to force it open another two feet. I stick my head in the crack. The room is eerily dark and quiet. Too quiet.

I push myself in through the small opening and scan the room. There is a hospital bed wedged up against door and something else on the floor, but it's too dark to make out.

Behind me, the nurse flicks on the light, pushing her way in as well.

My eyes pinch as they adjust to the harsh fluorescent lighting. Blinking my eyes into focus, I find her. She's curled up in a pool of her own blood. My heart jumps.

"Jada!" I cry, and rush to her side pulling her into my chest. Her head rolls back into the crook of my arm. Her face is no longer bandaged, so I can see the scar that runs down her beautiful face. I press my ear to her lips. There is only the faintest wheeze there. That's when I notice her arm is covered in blood.

She tried to kill herself.

"She's still alive," I scream at the nurse. "Save her! Please!" The nurse is paging for help and grabbing bandages from a cabinet.

Jada opens her one working eye at that moment and smiles up at me. She nuzzles her body closer into mine. She looks so happy, peaceful, and moments away from dying.

She closes her eyes in a smile before she goes limp in my arms.

***

The next few minutes pass in a haze of shouting and running. Doctors and nurses start pushing into the room. They try their best to get me out of their way, but I am unmovable. It's only when they discover that Jada's heart rate drops the moment I let go of her hand that they finally allow me to stay.

Things are happening so fast that it's hard to process what they are actually doing. At first, there was gauze, some sort of glue, and then even stitches to seal her wounds closed.

Because she lost so much blood, they have to give her a transfusion. Rather than leaving her to get the treatment, I curl up on the bed beside her, spooning her, never letting go of her IV-burdened hand. With each minute that passes, I can feel her getting stronger.

"Well, ain't you two just a sight."

I look up from the bed and find Kari glaring at me from the doorway.

"What are you doing here?" I ask. "I thought you hated hospitals."

"I do." She looks nervously around the room. "I drove your mom in. The plan was just to drop her off, but then I heard about what happened."

"Oh. Well, thanks for bringing her in. Where is she?"

She nods her head behind her. "The Docs are talking to her." Kari clears her throat. It's clear she doesn't want to be here. "They told me that you may have saved her just in the nick of time."

I nod, stroking Jada's hair.

"That's twice now this girl has been pulled back to stay among the living." Her eyebrows are pinched together, concentrating on something.

"And twice that your superstitions about us have been proven wrong." I can't help but add, "Every time we're apart, something bad happens. It's not the other way around like you think. We're meant to be together, Kari. I'm sorry it didn't work out for your friends, but we're not them."

She just shakes her head. "It seems all fine and good now, but the wheels are in motion. I can feel it in my gut."

Her comment sends a chill through me, but I refuse to let her upset me. I have other things to be worried about.

Just then, Jada moves in my arms. I hold my breathe.

A soft moan escapes her lips.

"Jada? Jada, can you hear me?" I cry.

"Where am I?" Her voice is weak, but I'll take it.

"I'll go get the doc," Kari says, backing out the door.

My heart begins to sprint seeing Jada's eye flutter.

"You're safe. I'm here. You're in the hospital," I say, sliding off the bed so I can look her in the eye. Her face has been re-bandaged and her arm is covered with gauze. She starts to panic a bit when she realizes her hands are strapped down.

"Shh, don't fight it. They tied your hands down so you won't..." I can't finish the thought.

Jada whimpers softly and the sorrow in her voice destroys me. I can't bear the thought that she might actually hate me for saving her.

"I'm sorry," I whisper. "I couldn't let you die."

She begins to sob softly before her eye drifts to her belly. "The baby?"

"Right as rain. This child is strong. Just like its mama."

She looks up at the ceiling as more tears run down her face. "Why? Why couldn't you just let me take care of this the right way?"

I carefully cup her face in my hands, forcing her to look at me.

"Because I can't live without you. If you die, I die. We're connected, Jada. You're my Twin Flame, just like Mr. Harper told us about in class. I know that now more than ever. When you slashed your wrist, I felt it. When I am away from you, I'm weak, but with you, I'm strong."

She looks at me for a second before she nods, "So you need me alive for selfish reasons." Her lips form a thin line. "That makes sense."

"No! Damn it, Jada!" I push off from the bed and start tearing at my hair. I'm explaining this all wrong.

Pacing the floor, I struggle to find my words. I have to tell her the truth. The truth of what's in my heart, to hell with the consequences. Walking back to the bed, I take her bandaged hand. Her eye locks on to me as I try to explain properly. "When you made that first incision, I felt it too. In here," I say pointing to my heart.

I expect her to start crying again but she doesn't. Instead, she starts laughing. "That's a very romantic lie, but that wasn't my first time." She turns her head away from me, as though ashamed.

My body tenses. "What do you mean this

wasn't your first time? Jada, have you tried to...kill yourself before?" My stomach lurches at the thought.

Jada rolls her head back to the center of her pillow and stares up at the ceiling. "No. This is a first for that, but it's not my first time cutting."

I cock my head, not sure of what to make of what she's just said.

"If I could take of my bandages, I'd show you. For the last ten years, I've carved my name into my arm. One letter a day."

The thought alone makes my stomach roll.

"Now you know how sick I am, so please. Please just go." Fat tears streak down her cheeks.

My hand grasps hers. "Never."

"Tobias, are you blind? Can't you see how messed up I am? Not just on the inside anymore. Now the whole world can see just how screwed up I am! Don't you get it? I can't bring a child into this world like this. Not looking the way I do, not thinking the way I do! God, why didn't you just let me die?"

The pain in her voice cuts into my soul.

"I didn't let you die because I'm not ready to lose you."

She looks up at me with her beautiful face, still bandaged and broken. She is by far the most beautiful thing I have ever seen.

"Why?" she whimpers.

"Because, I love you, Jada."

She rips her eyes off the ceiling to look at me. The expression she's wearing is nothing short of rage.

No! He did not just say he loved me. Bastard! Why is he lying to me? I pull my mutilated face out of his hands when he says it again.

"Stop it! Stop saying that!" I cry. Pity is the one thing I can't take right now, and that's all his proclamation of love is, pure and pathetic pity. His motive is crystal clear: give the girl who just tried to off herself a reason to live. But I am no fool.

"Just go. Leave me alone." I say. "Please."

Tobias stands up. I can feel his eyes on me but I won't look at him. I can't. I can't risk his eyes pleading with me to stay. Once he's gone, I can pick up the bits of me that remain and move on somehow. But I need to do it alone, away from people who knew me before. It's the only way I'll be able to stay sane.

I feel him get off the bed. His feet begin walking away towards the door.

My heart feels like it's breaking in two. I have to turn my head away so he won't see. He can't see this.

"I hate him," Tobias' voice seethes from across the room.

I turn my head to see that he hasn't left. Instead his feet are pacing the floor, his hands clenched into tight balls. His face is hot with anger.

"Don't hate him. It wasn't his fault," I sigh. "I seduced Hawk...I just don't remember it," I say, trying to believe my reasoning.

"That's not who I'm talking about, although I'm not overly fond of Hawk at the moment either!" he shouts. "It's your father that I hate!"

"Yeah, well, my father is dead, thanks to you guys. So you don't have to worry about him anymore either." Blaming him like that is a cruel card to play, but I need him to give up on me. I need him to move on. I'm no good to anyone anymore, not that I ever was.

"He may be gone, but he's still hurting you! Don't you see, Jada? He's convinced you that you can't be loved, and now that he's given you this scar, you actually believe him!"

My mouth opens to deny his accusation, but I can't. He's absolutely right.

He walks back over to me and kneels down to look at me. This time I can't seem to turn away from him.

"You think you're the only one who feels unlovable?" he asks, tears forming in his eyes. "I'm a walking death sentence, Jada. I was never supposed to live this long. All my life, the only people who were there for me are Hawk," he fights to get his name out, "and my mother. My mother, who had to adopt me because my own parents didn't want me." He looks up to the ceiling for a minute, as though he's trying not to cry. "For seventeen years, I've only had them." He looks down at my bed. "Other people don't want to risk getting close to me. They don't want to befriend someone they know they'll just have to say goodbye to."

His tears merge with mine on the bed below us. We share a common hurt.

"But I made it this long, Jada. I've made it. And now I know why. It's because I've been waiting to find you."

His hand closes around mine and my heart swells. I want to believe him so badly.

"But...I'm hideous," I start to say. Self-pity is threatening to consume me again.

"Jada, you are not hideous. You are more beautiful now than you have ever been. And I'm never leaving your side again. Do you hear me? Never. We are meant to be together. I can feel it in my bones in my lungs. When I'm near you...I'm home. For however long I have left on this Earth, I am going to be with you. Do you understand me?"

I stare at him though my one tear-soaked eye, needing to find the lie in his face, but I come up short.

"But this baby... *his* baby, " I can't even say his name.

"Hawk never has to know this child is his." Tobias squeezes my hand. "In fact, it's better if he doesn't know."

"Why?"

Tobias looks down at the bed. "Because if he knows, he'll hunt you down and claim you both." He looks up at me, panic in his eyes. "He can't take you away from me. Please, Jada. He'll never stop looking for you if he knows you have his child."

There is a genuine fear in his eyes, a fear that I can feel in my gut is the truth.

"Okay. He doesn't need to know." I whisper.

Tobias starts to cry in relief.

"I'll make you happy, Jada. I promise to God, I'll make you happy. Both of you."

Unable to resist, I smile. He really means what he's telling me. And for some foolish reason, so do I.

"Can I ask you for something?"

He lets out a small laugh. "Anything you want. It's yours."

"Kiss me?" I ask, my voice trembling, still expecting rejection.

Without hesitation, Tobias brings his hand to my face and cradles it in his hands. His fingers dig into my hair. He leans down to bring his lips to mine. As they connect, I am pulled back into myself. Pulled back to Earth. Pulled back to him. Closing my eyes to the past, I know that I am finally home.

Epilogue

Tobias

Looking around the apartment that is covered in bits of torn birthday paper, I can't help but smile. The afternoon sun is pouring into Ma's living room, making everything feel warm and perfect.

"Looks like someone had a good birthday, "I whisper to Jada, who is curled up on the couch, snuggling our daughter, Janelle. Her blonde curls mirror the exact color of her mother's.

My heart fills with such tenderness looking at Janelle's hand clasped tightly around her mother's neck as she sleeps on top of her. I'm amazed at how she isn't fazed in the least by her mother's scar. In fact, it's her favorite place to kiss her mama.

"Your mother spoiled her," Jada smiles back at me.

"I heard that," Ma says, coming in from the kitchen with a trash bag and a camera. "Grammies are supposed to spoil their grandchildren. It's the law." She puts the bag down and holds up her camera. It's the ancient digital kind. She likes to print out hard copies and frame them like they did in her day. I just shake my head at her stubbornness.

"Now, before we pick up this mess, give me a quick picture."

She snaps the picture of us cuddled up together. As soon as it's loaded, she walks over to her printer to make her precious copies.

Jada chuckles beside me. I nuzzle my nose into her hair, breathing her healing energy in. I haven't felt this alive in years, and it's all thanks to her and Janelle. They are my life now.

Across the room, Ma is cooing over her handiwork.

"Oh, he's gonna love this one," she whispers to the photo.

"Who is going to love it?"

Ma's smile vanishes as she puts the photo behind her back. "Um, no one honey."

She turns quickly and heads into the kitchen. Something doesn't sit right with me, so I follow behind her.

It's clear she's avoiding eye contact with me as she looks around the kitchen for something to busy herself with.

"Ma, what are you not telling me? Who are you showing this picture to?"

She puts her hands on her hips, the way she does when she feels like she's being attacked.

"Not that it's any of your business, but I've been writing to Hawk this past year."

"What?"

"Now don't get all upset. I feel bad for him. No one goes to see him, Tobias. Not even his parents." She raises her hand up to stop me from talking "I know that he killed Jada's father," she whispers, "but you both know that was to protect her." She shakes her head sadly. "Someone needs to let that boy know that he hasn't been forgotten about. And if his best friend wont do it, I will." She pushes past me to grab the broom from the closet.

My heart starts to thrum wildly in my chest.

"Ma," I say slowly, "does he know about Janelle?"

"Of course he does! Like I'm not gonna brag about my beautiful grandbaby! I send him pictures of you all every week. And don't you sass me about it. That boy ain't got nothing to look forward to locked away in that cell. He lives for the pictures of little Janelle. It's so cute the way he tears up when he sees her."

Of course he does.

Ma is blind to the fact that her granddaughter has the *exact* same eye color as Hawk. I don't think it's even dawned on her that he could even be the father. But you can bet your ass Hawk has it figured out. I've been praying everyday for her eyes to change color, as the doctor tells us will likely happen. That will been the only way we can stay. But now that he's seen her, we'll never be able to.

Now that Hawk knows she exists, he'd never let Janelle go. He'd take her from me, Jada, too.

My body goes numb. Ma leaves me in the kitchen with her broom, unaware of what she's done.

There is only one choice now. We have to run, before he gets out and tracks us all down.

End of Book Two

Danielle Bannister

Danielle Bannister is a work at home mom of two small children living in rural Maine. She has her BA in theatre and her Masters in Literary Education and working hard on several other novels. She has written the first in this trilogy, *Pulled*, as well as a collection of short works entitled *Short Shorts*. Her work can also be found in the 2012 edition of The Goose River Press Anthology and the 2012 Maine Writing Project's Anthology, *Writeous*. Pulled Back Again, the final installment of the Twin Flames Trilogy will be out soon.

You can follow her writing struggles on her website at: http://daniellebannister.wordpress.com/or find her on Facebook at: https://www.facebook.com/pages/Pulled-a-novel-by-Danielle-Bannister/127944507296637

Or Tweet her @getpulled